WICKE

P. H. Nix
Celeste Night

Cover: Nerd Sisters

Editing: Sneaky Ferret Editing

Proofreading: Marsha Bullock

First Edition

CONTENTS

For all the readers that see red flags and run... not because you're scared... but in the hopes you'll be chased

Playlist

Some songs that inspired us while we were working on this book!

Run On – Jamie Bower, King Sugar

Bottom of the River – Delta Rae

Bad Things – Jace Everett

Beat the Devil's Tattoo – Black Rebel Motorcycle Club

Raise Hell – Brandi Carlile

It Will Come Back – Hozier

Too Old to Die Young – Brother Dege

Hell's Bells – Cary Ann Hearst

Tear You Apart – She Wants Revenge

CODE MISTAKE – CORPSE, Bring Me The Horizon

Iko Iko – The Dixie Cups

AMERICAN HORROR SHOW – SNOW WIFE

way down we go (slowed + reverb) – badkarma

Dragula – Rob Zombie

Big Bad Wolf – In This Moment

Author's Note

Wicked Games is a horror romance where the main character will have more than one love interest eventually. This book ends in a cliffhanger. It contains dark themes, language, and explicit material that may not be for every reader. This book is for mature readers only. Please visit www.celestenight.com for more details.

Glossary of French Cajun Terms

Allons-Let's go

Bon chance - good luck

Cher- dear, sweetheart

Couillon-crazy, foolish

Envie-hankering

Gris-Gris - a curse

Laissez les bons temps rouler - Let the good times roll

Pauvre bête - poor thing (like bless your heart)

Rougarou-like a swamp werewolf

PROLOGUE

Four months ago...

Music pumped through speakers as Harper and I swayed our hips to the beat. Landry always threw some of the best parties, this one being no exception.

"Girl, slow down," Harper scolded as I chugged my mixed drink. Jungle juice always hit the spot. The key is to never eat the fruit. That's the shit that will have you fucked up, running ass cheeks out down the street.

"This is only my third cup," I retorted.

Harper Leigh was ever the true definition of a Southern belle. She barely cursed, was still a virgin who wouldn't go past first base, and attended Sunday services until night fell. It was one of the things that drew us together. Consider me the Yang to her Yin, or was it the other way around? *Shit, I'm buzzed already. They must've upped the alcohol-to-juice ratio this go-round.*

"Yeah, but you haven't eaten anything yet, remember?" she murmured, handing me a burger.

"Reason eight thousand, seven hundred and fifty-six of why I love you and you can never leave, Leigh," I slurred before taking a massive bite of food.

She rolled her eyes, knowing I was on the road to feeling way past drunk. I only called her Leigh when I was mad or wasted, and since I wasn't angry–drunk, it was.

"Drink this," she ordered.

I grabbed the bottled water from her proffered hand, or at least I thought I did. No water was in my grip.

Shaking her head, Leigh opened the water, put it to my lips, and I eagerly drank.

"Slow down, or you'll get sick," she scolded.

I mimicked her. "Okay, Mom!"

She snorted. "You'd be in the tub with a cold shower on if I was in full mom mode. Now take your damn time."

I opened my mouth to tease her about swearing when my phone buzzed in the back pocket of my cutoff denim shorts. Holding up the screen, I saw it was my brother, Minos. He texted and asked where I was. I shot off a quick reply and told him in not so many words to back off. I was at the Boutin's lake house with Harper and our friends. He replied with the middle finger and told me to be safe.

He was a pain in my barely-there ass, but I loved the broody dick.

"You good?" Harper asked. I dipped my chin, confirming everything was cool. I never spoke of family with her, even with our closeness. My family was involved in things that would blacken the soul of a regular person. I wasn't letting Harper anywhere near that. She was the light to my dark in this friendship, and I'd keep it that way.

Song after song played, and Harper and I danced like no one was watching us. At some point, Adeline joined, and I groaned. I really hated that bitch. Her skin should be neon green with how she envied Harper, her supposed best friend. And no matter how often I'd tell Harper about it, she'd brush me off and tell me Adeline meant no harm.

I wondered if Harper would think she meant no harm if she could see the way Addie rubbed on Landry's cock while she danced. With Landry squeezing her ass as he ground into her, I wouldn't be shocked if those two fucked behind Harper's back.

Conrad approached us, holding out two red solo cups. "You two need to catch up." He was the textbook definition of a pompous, jock fuckboy. He played football with Landry and Raymond for Archambault University. Conrad was barely six feet tall, with muddy brown eyes and hair to match. He was conventionally handsome if you went for the Abercrombie & Fitch look.

I didn't, not even remotely, which pissed him off to no end. He shouldn't be, though. I didn't like dick unless I was strapping one on to fuck the shit out of some girl. I told him this every time he made a move on me. My exact words were, 'Unless you have magically gained a cunt, you've got nothing to offer me.' I offered to top him at the last party. His eyes glimmered, and I knew he was about to say yes until Raymond called him to help him fuck the Benoit twins.

"Or y'all need to slow down," Harper suggested, taking her cup at the same time I took mine.

Conrad narrowed his eyes and watched intently as I took my first sip before he stalked off.

Harper lifted her cup to her mouth but paused before it touched her lips as the sound of *How Great Thou Art* blared like a police siren. She held her drink out to me as she stepped outside to take the call.

"Shit!" My head snapped toward my best friend as she walked back through the patio door moments later. Something terrible had to be up for her to cuss.

"Everything okay?" I sobered up immediately at the look on Harper's face.

Tears spilled down her cheeks. "It's Momma. I need to go."

"Do you want me to come with you?" I inquired, but knew the answer before she shook her head no. Her parents didn't take to me well at all. Can't say the feeling wasn't mutual.

For as long as I could remember, the Dubois hated me. They thought I was the spawn of Satan, which was fitting because my dad's name was Hades, but hilarious since Harper and I could pass for kin.

We both had long, wavy raven hair, a heart-shaped face with a button nose, and gunmetal eyes. But whereas I was tall with a lithe frame and porcelain skin, Harper was petite, curvy, and naturally tanned.

It probably had something to do with when they came to pick Harper up, and I was outside with my tongue down my ex-girlfriend's throat. I was the only exception to Harper's "good girl" disposition. She obeyed her parents in all areas unless it pertained to me.

"Text me to let me know you made it safely, and call me if you need me. I mean it, Harper Leigh. Don't make me drive to your house and beat down your door in the middle of the night. You know I'm good for it," I ordered, pecking her cheek before she dashed out of the house.

I peered down at the two solo cups in my hand. *To drink or not to drink? That is the question.* It didn't take long to come to an answer.

I chugged both back-to-back. The buzz was almost instantaneous.

Conrad reappeared with Raymond and Landry in tow. "Where'd Harper go?" Landry shouted over the music. He sounded like he was underwater, and his lips moved faster than I could comprehend.

When did more people walk over, and why were there two of each of these assholes?

Blinking, I attempted to refocus before I answered. "I think I need to get some air." My tongue felt funny as my words slurred. I definitely needed to go outside.

Frogs croaked as a summer breeze blew on my face, alerting me I made it to the deck by the lake.

My legs felt so heavy. "I jush needz to sith down," I mumbled, tittering. "Oushh," I grumbled, hitting the wood with a thud. Lights flickered in and out. "Whoze hells keepsh playing withs the lights?" I blinked a few times to realize it wasn't someone playing. It was lightning bugs.

I reached out to grab one and felt myself falling seconds before water seeped into my clothes. Gasping in shock, I swallowed lake water that burned my nose. I unsuccessfully fought to hold my breath as my lungs filled with the murky liquid.

Swim, you idiot.

My limbs wouldn't cooperate. I didn't attempt to push myself to the surface. My clothes acted as an anchor, weighing me down. I wanted to cry, but all the fight left my body. There was no preservation instinct to be found.

Maybe I just needed to rest my eyes for a while. Then I would swim.

"Holy shit! I think she's dead. Try harder," Landry barked.

Who's dead?

"No . . . no . . . no. This can't be happening," Conrad exclaimed.

What can't be happening? Why didn't anyone answer my damn questions? Everyone acted like they didn't hear me.

"I can't find a pulse. We've been at this for ten minutes. We need to call the police," Adeline shrieked.

"Are you out of your fucking mind? Did you forget my dad's the mayor, up for re-election this year? We can't afford to kill Hades's daughter," Landry barked.

Wait, who killed me? I'm not dead, you dick! Again, no one responded to me.

"Let's dump her back in the lake. The gators will get her, and we can deal with her car tomorrow. You're fucking lucky you kicked everyone out when you did," Adeline stated. "Or there's no way you'd be able to cover up that you drugged her."

Drugged?

"We can't hope the gators get her. What if they don't?" Landry whined.

"Go in the house and get the chicken we didn't bother grillin'. That'll bring em' for sure," Adeline instructed.

If I hadn't pieced together that these fuckers planned to kill me, I'd be impressed.

Move, you dumb bitch. Do something.

Why wouldn't my body cooperate? I growled, internally screaming and threatening to skin them all alive, then feed them to Gumbo.

I don't know how much time passed before they hoisted my body off the ground into the air.

"There's one now. I told you the raw meat would work. I'm surprised one didn't snatch her when she first splashed into the water."

"Shit, here comes another. They're coming out of the woodwork now. She'll be dealt with in no time."

I couldn't tell which idiot spoke over the pounding in my ears. My thoughts raced. I was about to die–they were about to kill me. All the things left unsaid. Harper was going to be pissed. My brothers would rain hell down on everyone involved. That was my only consolation as my body sank into the lake for the second time.

"Do we stay–."

Whatever, whoever was about to say cut off. My eyes shot open, and I wailed as sharp teeth lodged themselves in my stomach. The pain that sliced through my abdomen was unbearable.

"Fuck, she wasn't dead!"

I wanted to say no fucking duh, but it was too late. Seconds later, another set of jagged teeth latched onto my shoulder and tugged. The sound of ligaments and tendons separating from bone only amplified my torment.

Liquid filled my lungs as my arm was finally torn out of its socket. I didn't have a moment to catch my breath or fight before more teeth locked onto my left leg. It was like the gators were playing tug-of-war, and I was the rope.

All hope left me when jaws snapped open and clamped back down on my midsection. I was dying, and I knew nothing would save me.

"They're tearing her apart."

The last thing I heard before the final beat of my heart was, "Fucking brutal!"

Harper Leigh

Present Day

The lights of New Orleans fell away as the SUV sped down the road, and my heart beat faster the further from the city we got. Tucked inside my jacket sat the small black envelope, which felt like it weighed a million pounds rather than a few ounces. My fingers brushed along its edges, and I took a deep breath.

An icy chill ran through my veins when I found it waiting for me in my mailbox, and the room narrowed for a moment. Even as I ran my finger beneath the envelope's edge to open it, I knew my entire life would change once I saw its contents.

My imagination ran wild as I pulled the small, midnight-colored invitation out. Silver filigree adorned the edges of the textured paper, and I read the text twice to ensure I wasn't hallucinating.

I had jumped when Landry–the guy I had been dating for a little over two years—walked up behind me, putting his hand on my hip and peering over my shoulder. He commented in a playful tone that we should go, especially since three of our best friends had also received invitations. The words from the page were etched in my memory.

Dear Ms. Harper Leigh Dubois:

I formally invite you to a special House of Horrors grand opening. This event is by invitation only.

When: October 31 at 11 PM

Where: The Toussaint Manor

RSVP by texting "yes" to (504) 555-9676

At the very bottom of the invitation, someone wrote in pristine penmanship, "Be ready for the scare of your life."

Despite his reassurances, I couldn't shake the feeling that something was off. I tried convincing them I couldn't go. You would've thought my excuses were good enough between midterms, a fifteen-page paper, and work. They apparently weren't, and I succumbed to peer pressure.

When I was younger, my parents asked if my friends jumped off a bridge, would I follow them. The House of Horrors proved that I should have answered with a resounding yes.

That was why I sat nestled between the passenger side door and Raymond Hamilton while we sped down a bumpy road. Ray placed his arm around my shoulders, leaning close to me. The scent of his body spray made me queasy. "Don't worry, I'll protect you, Harper."

His hot breath washed over me, and I pressed my body against the door, trying to buy myself even a few inches. I gave him a fake smile, tossing my hair over my shoulder. He'd always made me uncomfortable. "I don't think that's necessary. It's a haunted house. That's not exactly a life or death situation."

He shrugged at me, and his grin widened. "Never know. It might really be haunted. Wouldn't want a ghost to get you."

I shuddered at his words, trying not to think about them. My family was superstitious and believed the veil between worlds was at its thinnest on Halloween. Coupled with my grandmother's adage of nothing good happening after midnight, I felt unsettled.

Part of me wanted to scream at Landry to stop the car, and I would find my way back to New Orleans myself. Surely, Uber could pick me up. Ray's fingers made circles on my shoulder, and I cringed. Why Addie insisted she had to sit in the passenger seat next to Landry was beyond me.

She claimed she needed to discuss a joint economics paper with him on the way but, so far, she hadn't mentioned anything about the project. I watched as her hand lingered on his arm just a little too long, or their gazes would linger. I tried to tell myself that it was simply unfounded jealousy on my part.

Landry had never given me any reason to doubt his loyalty to me. He was attentive and affectionate. He brought me flowers and sent me texts. In most ways, despite our heated arguments, I thought of us as the perfect couple, similar to my parents. Ours was the perfect relationship, one that would stand the test of time.

Adeline and I were friends at face value only, more frenemies than actual friends. And if it were up to me, I would never see Raymond or Conrad again. They were popular on campus, in fraternities, played sports, and were Landry's best friends from childhood, but something about them unsettled me. I only tolerated them for my boyfriend's sake, knowing they were a package deal.

An old-fashioned gas station was positioned on the left-hand side of the road, and the SUV careened into the parking lot before coming to a jarring stop. The gas station was small, painted in a washed-out yellow color with three rusty red and white gas pumps. A worn wooden sign hung over the entrance, warped and illegible.

"Hell yeah," Conrad whooped from the opposite side of the vehicle. "Beer stop."

I rolled my eyes and opened the car door, sliding out. The time on my phone was 10:15, and I was aggravated. Alcohol wasn't necessary for a haunted house, but in true frat boy fashion, everything was a party.

Neon lights caught my eyes, and my body drifted toward them unknowingly. Next to the rickety gas station sat a small house with purple siding—the Mirage. In bright pink, another sign advertised palm readings for twenty-five dollars.

"Where are you going, beautiful?" Landry yelled out, pulling me from my haze.

I waved at him and blew a kiss. "I won't be long. Can you get me a bottle of water?"

Addie laughed, walking backward toward the gas station's entrance. "You know that stuff is fake, right? Astrology, tarot cards, voodoo. They only work if you believe in them."

I ignored her and squared my shoulders, heading into the small shop. A bell chimed over the door as I opened it. My parents wouldn't have approved of my plans for the night. Not only was I out past curfew, but I was also visiting a palm reader. They always quoted scripture at me. *"Do not turn to mediums or necromancers; do not seek them out, and so make yourselves unclean by them."*

And their take on me going to a haunted house, well, that wouldn't exactly be favorable either.

I had never been more grateful that I was over eighteen and living in student housing for college. It afforded me a level of freedom I never had before.

The shop was dim, and candles sat on every surface, casting shadows on the wall. Mason jars containing various items lined a shelf. Red brick dust, grave dirt, and an assortment of dried herbs. Neat cursive labeled each item. In a small bowl, bones from an animal lay haphazardly. Crystals and stones of every color sat inside a curio.

A pang of sorrow hit me out of nowhere. Viola would have loved the shop. Halloween was her favorite holiday, and she obsessed over anything that dealt with the occult, magic, horror movies, or haunted houses. She would have dragged me to Toussaint Manor while telling Landry to fuck himself. That was just the way she was.

She had been missing for four months, and I tried to hope for the best. We went to a party together over the summer. It was the weekend that we discovered my mother was murdered, and I had gotten the phone call that night. She hadn't responded when I texted her the next day, looking for a distraction. I asked Landry what happened, and he told me Viola had left when everyone else had—nothing seemed out of place.

In twenty-four hours, I lost both my mother and my best friend.

A chill ran down my spine. The shop was unusually cold for that time of the year. I rubbed my arms and continued looking through the small shop's offerings. "Can I help you, child?" a voice asked from behind a gorgeous indigo velvet curtain, and I jumped. I had been so caught up in perusing the store's goods I had forgotten the real reason I had stepped inside.

"I saw you read palms, and I thought it might be fun," I replied, my voice smaller than I liked.

A woman stepped out from behind the curtain, a pipe in her hand. I couldn't determine her age from her appearance. Her skin was flawless, the color of copper, with small freckles that dotted the bridge of her nose and short chestnut hair twisted in tight coils on her head.

"Yes, I do. Come see," she said. She looked young, but her voice didn't quite match her face. It was warm and motherly, somehow ageless, and instantly put me at ease. The woman sat in a crimson velvet chair near a small table. On top sat a deck of cards I didn't recognize and another small bowl of bones.

I obeyed her command to come near, my feet shuffling forward of their own accord. Her hand was cold as she reached for mine, turning it up to glance at my palm. Her eyebrows furrowed, and her eyes glazed over as a single finger traced the lines on my skin like she was caught in a trance.

My breath hitched in my chest when she gasped. Suddenly, the nameless woman let go of me like I had burned her. "You need to go," she stated, her voice suddenly icy. "You have somewhere you need to be."

My eyes stung from the sudden shift in her demeanor, and I stepped back. "I need to pay you still," I said, trying to stall.

She shook her head and pointed to the door. "*Pauvre bête.* Now, out with you."

I turned on my heel and raced to the exit, pushing it open. The humid night air contrasted the cold interior of the shop, and my feet padded along the cracked concrete to Landry's SUV. Tears threatened to spill from my eyes. What had she seen in my palm? Was my future really that bad?

I clipped my seatbelt into place right as Landry and the others returned to the vehicle, joking around with each other. "That's not what your mom said last night," Conrad jabbed as he opened the door.

I wasn't in the mood to deal with them and didn't want to go to Toussaint Manor. For the briefest moments, I'd forgotten why we were even this far from New Orleans. That bubble had vanished, and doubt and anxiety lingered in its stead.

Addie gave me one look and scoffed. "I told you not to go, Harper. You're always so sensitive. What? Did an old woman hurt your feelings? Tell you that you'd die alone because you're still a virgin?"

Landry gave her a look I couldn't decipher. "Shut the fuck up, Adeline. Leave her alone and drink your tequila." He pulled a water bottle from his brown bag and handed it to me. "Ignore whatever the fortune teller told you. I'm sure it's not true."

I wiped at the back of my eyes but said nothing, choosing to focus on the water. That was the thing. I couldn't explain why I was upset. The fortune teller hadn't said anything to me. Not really. "Can you guys take me home?"

The bad feeling from earlier had returned, multiplying. My brain screamed at me I should just go home and hide beneath my blankets. Raymond pulled out a fifth of whiskey next to me and turned the bottle up, making it bubble. He nudged me with his shoulder. "Harper Leigh, you're not going home. Tonight is going to be amazing. You just wait and see."

I pressed my cheek against the cool glass and stared out the window, hoping he was right but knowing he wasn't. On top of being a creep, Ray was an idiot. The engine started, and the car pulled back out onto a highway.

Ten minutes later, at 10:52, the private driveway for the Toussaint Manor came into view. Rusting wrought iron fencing encompassed the estate, but the gates were thrown open. Lightning flashed in the sky, and clouds rolled in, a storm brewing in the distance. Despite the laughter and conversation, I could hear thunder rumbling.

My heart beat faster as we barreled down the road lined by willow trees dripping with Spanish moss. The limbs were contorted, sweeping across the path from age and the wind howling through them. Then they finally gave way, and the mansion came into view. Terror clawed at my stomach. It looked like something that was pulled straight out of my nightmares.

There was no way they would convince me to step foot inside.

The structure was a crumbling relic of days long past. Once upon a time, it had been white, but age and neglect left the paint cracked and graying. The columns lining the porch were covered by ivy, and the windows were cracked, thin web-like veins adorning them. The house seemed to groan and creak from the incoming storm as the weather vane spun wildly.

Bile rose in my throat, and I swallowed it down when Landry opened the door. "This is so fucking cool," he shouted. Everyone exited the vehicle one-by-one until I was the last one sitting, staring at Toussaint Manor as lightning illuminated it.

"Don't be a pussy, Harper," Raymond stated, grabbing my wrist.

Pain lanced up my arm from his pressure on the joint, and I winced. "I don't think this is a good idea," I pleaded with him, hoping at least one person would side with me. My papa would have called me a *couillon* three times by this point.

Addie glared at me and placed a hand on her hip. "Harper, haunted houses are all fake. They'll probably have some fake blood inside and a few actors wearing clown masks. Besides, don't you have some holy water or something in your purse? Jesus will protect you," she mocked.

I bit down on my bottom lip and clutched my water bottle like an anchor, sliding out of the SUV. Addie was just being a bitch like usual, so I kept my mouth closed.

Everyone assumed I was fervently religious, like my parents, but it couldn't be further from the truth. Sometimes, late at night, I wondered if anyone was truly out there listening to my prayers. Sure, I was a virgin, but that wasn't because I was waiting for marriage. Things just hadn't felt right yet.

Landry walked up to me and put his arm around my shoulders. "Don't listen to her right now, baby. The house just looks creepy as hell."

His touch helped ease at least some of the apprehension that had taken up residence under my skin, and when he laced our fingers, I thought everything would be alright. Fifteen minutes in a haunted house. I could live through anything for fifteen minutes.

We walked together across the lawn, dead grass crunching beneath our shoes. The air was salty from the storm, but it didn't mask the underlying decay of the property. Lightning flashed against the black sky again in quick succession. A fat drop of water landed on my face as we ascended the steps. One gave way beneath my foot, and I stumbled forward before Landry caught me.

A sign stood on an easel next to the front door. "Please place all cell phones and electronic devices in the provided basket." Another thing that I had misgivings about, but one by one, they placed their phones in the small wicker basket lying beside the door. Conrad grinned at us. "You know what this means, right? I bet they have some awesome animatronics!"

I stared at him blankly. I doubted that was what it meant. The kid's pizza joint didn't make me leave my cell phone at the door, and they had tons of animatronics. I pushed all of those thoughts from my head and turned to the house.

The door itself was recently painted crimson, a stark contrast to the rest of the structure. I took a deep breath and turned the handle. The screech of the hinges echoed, drowning out the thunder, and I stepped inside.

The foyer was a long, narrow corridor that looked abandoned, and cobwebs hung in the corners of the vaulted ceiling. Wood paneling, dark from age, covered the walls, and an oak sideboard sat in the corner, dust covering the top in a thick layer. The air felt stale, like no one had lived there in at least a hundred years.

"This is amazing," Conrad said as he ran a finger through the dust, drawing a lopsided penis.

Suddenly, something clicked behind us, echoing in the hallway. My heart skipped a beat as my mind raced, and I turned back to the door. It sounded like it bolted shut on its own. I tried the handle, attempting to turn it. Nothing. I pulled on it, hoping it was just stuck.

A deep voice came over a sound system of some type. "Welcome to Hell. We're so glad you came to join our game tonight." Laughter crackled through the air as goose bumps formed on my skin. *"Laissez les bons temps rouler."*

EREBUS

On the computer monitor, I watched as chaos ensued. The three guys, all clean-cut and dressed in polo shirts with designer jeans, laughed as the girl, who looked like a doll, crossed her arms over her chest. She was clearly not amused.

The one that was the most interesting had hair as dark as the night, and she tugged at the front door, probably praying that there was a way out of my web. Hint: there wasn't. The only escape was completing our trials, and none of them would leave Toussaint Manor alive.

Her terror was delicious and exciting, sweeter than the pralines on the desk in front of me. Absentmindedly, I petted Gumbo on the head. He grumbled and laid his head down, disappointed that he wasn't the center of my attention. "Shh, cher. Let me work for a while."

Minos stared at me, taking a sip from his coffee cup. "You treat the gator better than you do most people."

"Says the asshole with two killer teacup yorkies with more outfits than a debutante." The two demon mutts yipped from their dog beds. "Plus, gators have souls. Dear *Maman* taught us that."

I grinned wider, swiveling in my chair to face him, and pointed at the screen. "This is my favorite part. Seeing the look on their faces when they realize it's not just a game. This group isn't very bright. They think it's all a joke still."

My brother ran a hand down his face, exasperated as usual. "In the next five minutes, they'll know the truth." He raised an eyebrow at me. "Besides, it seems that Harper Leigh has already figured it out."

Even as we spoke, Harper's eyes darted around the foyer, looking for an exit. Her fingers clawed at the door as she snapped at her friends. "This isn't funny!"

She was wrong about that, but I wouldn't correct her. Not yet.

Even through the feed, she was beautiful. Wild looking. Her lips were parted, and I knew her pupils were blown from the fear coursing through her body. If you looked close enough, you could tell that her soul had a sliver of darkness just begging to come out and play. What better holiday than Halloween to make that happen?

My dick grew hard in my pants watching her, and I palmed it through the fabric. "It's such a shame," I mused out loud. "I want to keep her. Please, just this one, Minos."

She would be the perfect addition to our little family. I could teach her everything she needed to know and mold her into what I wanted her to be. Gumbo wouldn't be happy sharing my attention, but–

My brother sighed at me, cutting off my thoughts. For a fraction of a second, I assumed he might agree to my request. After all, I didn't ask for a lot. "No, Erebus. We can't keep her, and you know why. She's not a pet, and it's against the rules. Besides, she won't make it through tonight. They never do. You can have fun with her, but then she dies. Just like the others."

Fuck the rules. I was sick of them. I tried to plead with him. "But what if–"

He cut me off with a look. "There are no buts. Besides, even if she does live, you wouldn't want her after the trials. The pretty girl you see on the screen isn't who will emerge from the house."

He was wrong, but I stopped the conversation. There was no point in continuing it, but I knew the truth. I wanted Harper Leigh for myself, even if she had burns or scars. Even if she was missing fingers. All of those were genuine possibilities. She was my perfect plaything, and she didn't know it. I could make her into the nightmare she was destined to be.

Finally, I hit the button on the sound system, knowing it was time to start the next stage of our game. "*Bonjour, mes amis.* I'm sure that you're curious about why you're here tonight. How did you find yourself in our web?"

"Fuck you," my little nightmare screamed at the wall. "Let us out."

I let out a deep chuckle. "Shh, cher. Don't be so hasty. I think you'll enjoy the games we have planned for you." Gumbo grumbled at my feet again, and I gave him a reassuring pat before continuing. "Now, as I was saying. At the beginning of each room, I'll play a video that contains a clue about why you're here."

"What's the catch?" Harper shouted. Her friends were still laughing, not taking the situation seriously. They would soon.

"The catch is that you have to survive to find out why."

I pressed play on the computer beside me, sending the video feed to the screen positioned further down the hallway, right outside the entryway for the first game. My heart caught in my throat as I watched it alongside them, and sorrow coated my tongue.

It was a picturesque summer day. The sun glowed in the azure sky, and puffy white clouds rolled overhead. The grass was still green, not dry from the heat yet. Tall trees sat in the distance, their leaves swaying in the gentle breeze. Sunlight glimmered off of the lake water like diamonds.

From the visual on the screen, you could almost smell honeysuckles and hear the scream of cicadas in the background. That weekend would change the trajectory of their lives for everyone involved, but they didn't know it yet.

Three girls were dressed in shorts, wearing bikini tops, sitting on colorful beach towels, smiling as they chatted about whatever girls that age discuss. Occasionally, one would throw her head back in laughter, and another would raise her eyebrows.

One by one, three guys appeared in the frame. One flopped down beside the curvy black-haired beauty and tugged her into his lap. Another pestered the woman holding a book, and she shoved at his chest, rolling her eyes at his antics. The third ran past everyone, jumping into the crystal water of the lake.

It was a moment torn straight out of a teen movie. Too bad it took a sinister turn.

I cleared my throat, ignoring the emotion that clogged it. "Now, if all contestants can enter door number one, the games can begin."

I watched as Harper entered the room and held my breath, hoping she wouldn't be the first one to go. Perhaps I could convince my brother to keep her if she survived.

HARPER LEIGH

N o one else seemed to recognize the severity of the situation. We were locked inside, and according to the voice—the only way out was to live through the games they had planned.

I stepped through the door into what appeared to be a grand hall, or what used to be one. Dull, thick burgundy curtains you could tell were once rich in color lined the length of the wall. I crossed the expanse of the grimy carpet, nearly tripping on the cracked, checkered ballroom floor. Curtains meant windows, and windows meant a way out.

Swerving around overturned wooden tables, I strode across the room and yanked the drapery back, only to be met with plexiglass bolted over a window painted black. Pane after pane turned up the same.

"Why are you doing this?" I screamed, knowing whoever orchestrated this was watching and listening.

"Harper, baby, calm down. This is all in good fun, just like the invitation promised," Landry crooned as he pulled me into his muscular chest.

It was moments like this that made me miss Vi even more. She'd be helping, not knocking back bourbon from a flask kee-kee'ing like idiots who die first in horror movies. At the thought of my best friend's name, my chest tightened.

Turning in Landry's arms, I lifted my gaze and asked, "What was the video about?" The more I thought about it, the more I wondered why they'd chosen the day of the party—the day Vi went missing. I'd been so lost in my grief from the loss of my mother that I barely processed the reason they'd said she left.

He paused, peering at where Raymond, Addie, and Conrad stood bunched together by the candlelit sconces. As he shifted his attention back to me, I noticed blush-pink lipstick, the same shade Adeline wore tonight, on the side of his neck.

"It's nothing, Harper," his tone chilled. "Just whoever's planned this is trying to add some mystery and build tension to the night. Shit, I wouldn't be surprised if it was Viola behind this," he answered, lowering his mouth toward mine.

I stepped back. Vi told me time and time again of her suspicions of Addie and Landry, but I didn't believe her. Landry had been the epitome of a Southern gentleman. He never pushed me too far, and respected my decision to wait for marriage. He attended service with me each Sunday, and never let me walk on the side of the sidewalk closest to the street.

Landry's brows scrunched up in confusion. "What is it, baby?"

My mouth parted to confront him when the voice from the sky interrupted.

"One should never start rigorous activities without stretching. So, let's warm up."

The doors we came through swung shut, and a metal sheet slammed down, trapping us. Addie shrieked and began running in Landry's direction before latching onto Conrad's arm.

"Still think this is all just some silly game?" I snapped, pulling from his arms.

Before Landry could reply, a voice different from the one we heard when we arrived spoke. "Now, I need everyone lined up at the edge of the dancefloor. You have ten seconds."

I scrambled to follow his instructions, dragging Landry by his arm.

"Ten . . . nine . . . eight," an automated voice began.

"You really are being dramatic, Harper Leigh. Nothing will happen," he said once we stood where the carpet and tile met.

"Seven . . . six . . . five . . . four."

Addie's eyes flitted around the room before dashing to the spot next to Landry, and I stepped between them. When her blue eyes met mine, fear was clear in their depths. It appeared she finally recognized the world of shit we might be in.

"Three . . . two . . ."

Raymond arrived next, a cocky grin pasted on his face.

"I don't know why y'all are acting like a bunch of scared pussies," Conrad snorted as he stood across the room. Conrad's brow arched in challenge as his lackadaisical posture signaled his defiance.

"One."

Turning, I gasped as ten square holes opened in the walls, five on each side. My mouth hung open as ball launchers emerged through the openings.

The machine directly behind Conrad pulled back, and I watched in horror as a ball of fire hurdled through the air in what felt like slow motion until it connected with his arm.

Conrad shrieked, trying to put out the flame. The scent of burning flesh that permeated the room proved he hadn't been fast enough.

"Holy shit," Raymond shouted as Conrad pulled his polo off, desperately attempting to extinguish flames creeping up his limb.

Landry burst into action, pulling off his jacket as he ran toward our friend.

"Now that we understand how this works. Let's get started," said the voice I'd dubbed Jack. The other person was Jim. They both shared a smooth timbre, but one was more smokey than the other. "We're going to play Red Rover."

"I don't remember there ever being fire in that game," I quipped.

A deep chuckle came over the sound system as Landry walked over with a still whimpering Conrad. His arm was raw, and parts of his shirt melted in the flesh. Bile churned in my stomach. That had to be at least a second or third-degree burn. I could see the white of his forearm.

"Now, where's the fun in playing it like we did when we were *enfant* still on our *Maman's* teet, cher?" Jim asked. Amusement was clear in his tone.

Jack cut in, "We'll say, Red Rover, Red Rover let, followed by whatever we want to be called over. If you fit what's called, you need to make it to the other side of the floor while you dodge flaming tennis balls."

Raymond's throat cleared. "There weren't no goddamn tennis balls in that game!"

"If you haven't figured it out yet, let me help y'all. We make our own rules, and y'all have to follow them if you want to get out of here alive," Jack snapped. "We decided to marry Red Rover to the game of burn. Now get ready, unless you intend on ending up like the snot-faced asshat who thought his britches were too big to follow simple instructions."

I gulped down my snark and readied myself for whatever came next.

"Red Rover, Red Rover, let purple come over," Jim instructed.

"Fuck," I heard Addie whisper. She was wearing a purple t-shirt.

I peered to my left and right to see if anyone would join her on the run, but she was it.

"You've got this, Addie," I encouraged. I wasn't a fan of hers, but that didn't mean I wanted her dead.

Addie sprinted, dodging ball after ball until she reached the other side. Flames danced past her midair, and initially, I thought she would remain untouched. At the last second, she whimpered as she collided with the wall, touching her hand to her cheek. On it, a blister was forming. The once flawless skin she'd prided herself on having was now singed, like the top of a crème brûlée. "You'll pay for this," she shrieked at the ceiling as tears rolled down her face. But I knew her threats had fallen on deaf ears. What did she really think she could do to the men who had yet to make an appearance?

The fragrance of smoke filled the room. I turned, noticing one of the old curtains had caught fire.

"Aren't you going to put that out?" Landry barked, pointing to the steady flame spreading.

"Nope, and if you don't want to be human s'mores, I'd suggest you shut the fuck up and play. The house will be fine, but you won't," Jack growled.

My heart pounded as smoke filled the room, and I waited for Jim or Jack to give the next command. I'd had a terrible feeling ever since laying eyes on the invitation, and now I knew why. I might not make it out of the Toussaint Manor alive. Jack and Jim were certifiably insane.

"Red Rover, Red Rover, let people with black hair come over," Jim commanded, amusement lacing his voice. This really was all a game to him. My eyes watered from the smoke, and bits of ash floated into the air. The temperature in the room had increased, causing sweat to form on my brow.

Time slowed as my legs pumped, and I prayed I could make it to the other side unscathed. Even the sound was muffled, though I heard Landry call out my name in encouragement. He could go screw himself with Addie's lipstick staining his skin. If we ever made it out, I would have to tell him what I thought.

I peered ahead. I was almost there. Inhaling, I took a few more steps, then shifted my gaze left and right at the familiar whooshing. I dropped to the floor as two balls flew toward me from opposite directions, one aimed at my head and the other at my torso. "Shit," I muttered as I hit the ground with a thud.

"Get up, baby. There's more coming, Harper. You gotta move now," Landry bellowed, and three more tennis balls shot from the wall. That's when I noticed the machines shot not only straight, they adjusted based on our movements.

"For fuck's sake," I snapped and stood. I darted forward, dodging three more balls as sweat trickled down the back of my neck. I screamed when bright orange and yellow flames with the potent scent of gasoline zipped past my nose.

A few more paces to go.

The heat from another fireball whirred by my head, causing me to gasp, and the stench of burning hair hit my nose. I'd never felt more grateful when I made it to the other side, my body colliding into the wall with a thud, and I slid to the floor. Gingerly, I reached up and touched the edge of my singed lock. I could hide it in a ponytail, but it pissed me off.

It could have been worse than just an inch of hair.

Round after round, we played, smoke burning my lungs and eyes. The room was an inferno, and ash danced in the air. Flames consumed everything in their wake, and I wondered how we had managed to stay alive. The blaze had cast everything in an orange glow. Coughing filled the air, adrenaline the only thing keeping me going. Sweat covered my skin from the intensity of the heat.

When would this portion of their game end? We wouldn't survive much more of this. "Last round," Jim stated, answering my unspoken question. I wanted to sigh in relief. It was just Landry, Ray, and me left on this side. We'd all been back and forth a few times.

"Red Rover, Red Rover, let friends of Vi come over," Jack demanded.

I detected a hint of anger at the growl of Vi's name. *Did this have to do with her?* But there wasn't time to decipher that. I shot from my spot, then ducked and dodged each ball. One flew right in front of my face just as the other side of the room came into focus.

"Ahhh," Raymond wailed. "Help," he pleaded, but as I whirled around from the safety zone and saw him, I knew it was too late.

He'd been pegged three times. Ray's pant leg, shirt, and hair were ablaze, and the balls just kept landing. One flew right into his crotch with such force that he was thrown backward. His head whipped toward us, giving us an unobstructed view as his skin bubbled and then curled, melting away the tissue. Before his next cry, Ray slumped to the floor. Fire covered his entire body like he was nothing more than kindling. His once luxurious hair–*gone.* The muscular physique he boasted about–*melted.*

I snatched Landry's jacket and darted forward. "We have to do something. We can't just sit here and watch him burn," I shouted.

Landry's arm wrapped around me, yanking me into his chest. "There's nothing we can do, baby. He's too far gone." I wiped away the tears running down my face. They felt cold compared to the tight dryness of my skin as I watched on in despair. There was no way to save him, and no way out of the room. We all stood frozen as our friend burned, writhing on the floor, desperately attempting to put out the fire consuming his body. His screams would haunt me for eternity, as would the scent of burning flesh and hair. The carpet at the edge of the tile caught on fire as Addie fell to her knees. In a last-ditch effort, as his body went into fight mode, Ray pushed from the ground and dove in our direction, falling five feet from us.

The charred smell was far worse than Conrad's earlier. Raymond's body jerked before going still, the skin left blackened from the fire. Pieces of bone peeked through in places, and a wave of nausea hit me as the crackling sound of his flesh cooking echoed off the walls. It sizzled like the bacon Mawmaw made on Saturday mornings when I slept over.

I had never been close to Raymond, and I wouldn't say I liked his leering gazes, but I had also never wished he died. I turned and emptied the contents of my stomach from the horror of what I had just witnessed just as the door behind us swung open.

Jack's voice played over the sound system. "Congratulations. If you're hearing this, it means you live to play another round. Proceed to the other room or stay and enjoy some barbecue."

Determination steeled my spine, and I walked to the exit, desperate for fresh air. If I wanted to discover why the hell I was here, I needed to live through their twisted games. If I lost, the cost would be my life.

Minos

"That last part, Minos—enjoy some barbecue," Erebus cackled and brought up the images on the computer. "The horrified looks on their faces as that asshole burned—fucking priceless."

He zoomed in on the raven-haired beauty that oozed innocence, but I could see it in her silver eyes. Harper Leigh had the glint of darkness brewing below the surface, and I was going to force it out of her. I watched as he hit print. That photo was going in the spank bank. I couldn't say I blamed him. "Print me a copy too," I commanded.

The camera feed rolled as they stood in the hallway, waiting for further instructions.

"Why would they do that?" The annoying blonde said.

She'd have died in the first round if I'd had my way. The things she did behind Harper's back with that boyfriend were more than enough reason to carve out her reproductive organs and decorate the house for Christmas.

"You think once Harper discovers what snakes her boyfriend and best friend are, she'll take part in the torture room?" I murmured. The idea of Harper using a bone saw across Adeline's abdomen before she was divested of her uterus made my cock hard.

Erebus spun around, bouncing on his gamer chair, and clapped his hands like he just won the prize of a lifetime. "That'd be better than head from Lacey."

My eyes widened in surprise. Lacey was Erebus's favorite girl—at least for the moment. She'd been around a lot longer than the other girls. I peered down at the braided bracelets he never took off until it was time to add a new girl.

"Does that mean Lacey will join the ranks?" I questioned, pointing to his wrist.

He rubbed each of the five with a loving caress. His attention focused on the ginger band. Amelie, his first infatuation. Erebus stalked her for months before he brought her home. It took a few more for her to fall and even less for her to be replaced. He'd mourned her for a year before a new girl appeared.

"If she lives," he replied and turned back to the monitors.

My thoughts sobered at the reminder. Harper Leigh wouldn't live. She took someone from us, and for that, she and her friends would die. I was pissed at myself for even suggesting it. I'd take the picture Erebus printed and use it for target practice. Vi didn't deserve what happened to her, and in my mind, Harper was the guiltiest of them all. She was her best friend—almost like sisters.

"Open the room so we can get the next trial started," I instructed, and Erebus's fingers flew across the keyboard.

The Landry douche grabbed Harper and pulled her into his side. "You don't go first this time. Suppose it's rigged to shoot spears or some shit?"

I made a mental note to add that to the list. *A twisted version of ring toss, maybe?* That had potential, but needed some work.

"So, who do you think should go first since your precious Harper Leigh can't?" Adeline hissed. Her face blossomed red at the obvious slight. She opened her mouth to speak, but I won't have her fuck with what was planned.

"Enter the next room, or I'll release the dogs," I ordered, then lifted my finger from the mic and picked up Pollo. Artie whined from his bed. I probably should've let them be. They'd played nice with Gumbo all night.

I sighed and scooped him up as everyone filtered into the adjoining space. The monitor was already on. Erebus waited until everyone stood in front of it before he hit play.

The sky was on fire, cast in a kaleidoscope of brilliant hues of oranges, pinks, and purples. The lake reflected back the heavens, ripples occasionally breaking up the picture. It was the perfect end of a summer's day. The sound of frogs and cicadas filled the evening air.

No one knew soon it would be marred by tragedy.

Only two of the women and two of the men remained, sitting near the water's edge while they sipped from red plastic cups. From the camera's angle, you could see everyone's face more clearly, and it was notable how closely the women resembled one another.

Both had smiles plastered to their faces, and the one threw her head back in laughter at something they were quietly discussing, a secret between just the two of them. Suddenly, one man lifted the girl whose book had been sitting in her lap, and a squeal pierced the air.

He took off into a run with her in his arms toward the water.

The video ended, and I studied their reactions. Addie's eyes darted quickly between Conrad's and Landry's. Both gave her an almost imperceptible shake of their heads. One I would've missed if I hadn't been observing them. Their guilt was evident–painted on every part of their features.

"We're going to draw out their deaths," I growled, and Erebus grunted his agreement.

The death of their friend had done nothing to quench my thirst for vengeance. I wanted to gut them, each in a more violent way than the last. They would beg for mercy, but that bitch couldn't save them–not for what was coming next.

"Why do they keep showing clips from the night at the lake house?" Harper asked, garnering my attention.

Why was she confused? She was there. It's why she would die.

Harper peered up into the corner as if she knew precisely where the cameras were. Her gun-metal eyes narrowed as her nose scrunched in confusion.

"They're sick fucks," Landry shouted. He lifted his hand and gently guided Harper's face to his. "This is part of some twisted game." I was tempted to end him now. The pretty boy mayor's son. He'd soon learn just how sick we were, and how twisted the games they'd face would be.

Harper opened her mouth to speak, but Landry pressed a kiss to her lips and silenced whatever question laid on the tip of her tongue. My teeth clenched. Watching him touch her filled me with irrational anger.

Annoyed, I slammed my fingers on the microphone. "Proceed to the next room," I snarled. Harper jumped back, pulling herself from Landry's embrace.

"Someone's getting testy," Erebus teased.

"Just shut the fuck up and run the next trial," I snapped, and he snickered.

I watched as they entered the adjoining space and reminded myself none of them would survive the night. Harper Leigh was nothing more than a dead bitch walking.

Harper Leigh

S cenes from the two video clips played on a loop in my mind as we entered the new space. *What did that night have to do with why we were here?*

I was jolted from my thoughts when the door slammed behind us, and the telltale sound of gears signaled the metal sheet was being lowered. We were trapped once again.

Landry grabbed hold of my hand and pulled me into his side. "Stay close," he instructed.

I wanted to press him for answers, but Conrad's shocked gasp stole my attention. "What the fuck is that smell?" he bellowed.

Turning, I surveyed the room. It looked like some sort of indoor pool area. A metal lid lay over the large rectangular area, but the scent of chlorine was absent from the space. In its place was the pungent aroma of mildew and death.

I lifted my arm in an attempt to block out the stench, then continued to look around. Like the ballroom, this room was also dilapidated. Greenery of some sort grew in the cracked stone flooring surrounding the pool. The once white paint, now beige and covered in grime, peeled from the walls, and the floor-to-ceiling windows were sealed over with sheets of wood at least three inches thick.

Once again, there was no way out.

"Bitches and punks, please take your places on both sides of the pool. I strongly suggest that you pair up–one dick and one pussy on each team, or I'm sure this will be over before it even truly gets started, and that would be a fucking shame," Jim singsonged through the sound system.

"Landry's with me," Addie blurted, and I rolled my eyes, preparing to pull from his side.

His grip tightened. "Are you dumb?" Landry snapped at her. "Why the hell would I partner with you and leave Harper with Conrad?"

I'd say it was the question of the evening if it weren't for the clusterfuck we found ourselves in. I couldn't even bask in the chastised look on her annoyed face. Addie's cheeks bloomed red, her lips thinning once she noticed my attention was on her.

"It's not fair for me to have a one armed partner." She gestured to the wound on Conrad's arm. "Whatever. Conrad, you're with me. Let's get this over with," she exclaimed, and as she strode around the pool to the other side closest to the windows, I swore she mumbled she hoped I'd die next.

Landry kissed the top of my head, and I had to fight not to smash him in the face. Something was going on, and I was the only one out of the loop. We were here because of that night at his family's lake house. They'd all behaved differently after that. Something I would've usually questioned if I wasn't lost in grief.

Huffing, I allowed myself to be tugged over to our side, finally noticing the large rope placed across the pool.

The stench from this spot made me gag. "We'll probably pass out from the smell before whatever these psychopaths have planned," I choked out.

"Well, that's not very nice, Harper Leigh. What would your folks say about you judging people?" Jim jested.

Telling him to fuck off was on the tip of my tongue, but I swallowed the retort, biting the inside of my cheek. The tang of copper slid down my throat. It was better to swallow blood than to anger these two sick fucks.

"Now I know y'all have played a round of tug of war at least a few times in your pathetic lives. Still, I'll give a brief refresher and then explain the object of the game," Jack stated.

If ever there was a time I was happy to be cornbread fed, it was now. Conrad was just shy of six feet and stocky, the perfect size for his nose tackle position. A strong gust off the coast could blow away Addie. On the other hand, Landry was over six feet tall and had two hundred pounds of lean muscle. Whatever this game turned out to be, my money was on us winning.

"When I say get ready, y'all are gonna pick up that rope. Then, when you hear the horn, you'll tug for your life, literally. The game doesn't end until one of you lands in the pool," Jack explained.

Conrad snorted, "What's the catch? After the last game, I don't believe for a single second it's that easy."

Nodding, I hummed my agreement. There was definitely more to this. Jack's instructions were far too simple.

"I guess you're not a dumb jock after all. Pick up the rope," Jack commanded. Jack was the asshat in this deadly duo. He was brusque and delivered his vitriolic words venomously.

"I'll anchor," Landry offered. "That should give us more leverage."

Addie watched, then turned and whispered something in Conrad's ear. He nodded, taking the same position as Landry. Having your strongest person on anchor is a beginner strategy in this game. I didn't know why she'd need to try and keep that a secret.

"Clock's ticking. You have one minute to get into your position before the game starts, with or without you. I strongly recommend you don't let that be the case," Jack snapped.

Bending, I grabbed the rope and then quickly dropped it. "Fuck," I shouted, twisting to see the slivers of cuts in my hand. "Glass?" I barked. "You put glass in the goddamn rope!"

"That's not very godlike, Harper Leigh," Jim tsked. "What's that? Ten Hail Mary's?"

"Wrong denomination, asshole," I quipped. I never wanted to stab a person in the eye so badly. The way he joked so easily when our lives were on the line stoked the rage in me I'd worked so hard to hide. "Breathe, Harper Leigh," I murmured low enough that only I could hear.

No one moved to lift the rope. We all stood there, trying to find another way. I searched the room to no avail, hoping to find something to protect our hands. If we played their way, it would embed shards of glass into our palms.

Sighing, I began to lift my shirt before a hand halted my movements.

"What are you doing?" Landry questioned.

I twisted, narrowing my gaze. "Wrapping my shirt around my hands."

"But they'll see you topless," Landry snapped. My nostrils flared. He couldn't seriously be worried about whether my tits were on display. I'd strip naked if it got us all out of this hellhole.

"Better to see my bra than to shred my palms," I argued through clenched teeth.

Landry's face flushed beet red with indignation, a rebuke on the tip of his lips.

"Thirty seconds," Jack declared, ending all discussions.

Wasting no more time, I yanked my shirt over and wrapped my hands as best as possible. Landry followed suit once he realized there was no other option, and when I gazed across the room, I noticed Addie and Conrad did the same. Conrad wrapped the rope around the waist of his jeans, desperately trying to compensate for the arm that had been injured.

I picked up the rope just as the horn sounded, and the cover of the pool slid open. Clear water revealed bright lights in a shiny underground metal pool. "Who designed the pool to be like the giant jambalaya cooker from Coop's in the French Quarter?" I twisted and whispered in Landry's ear.

He shrugged, puzzled by the sight in front of us. "We can worry about that after I ensure you and I make it out of this room. Now focus, Harper Leigh," Landry ordered. "If someone has to die in this room, it won't be one of us."

Spinning back around, I peered into the deceptively still water. I knew Landry was right, but something niggled in the back of my mind. There was no familiar chlorine fragrance. In fact, outside of the decay, I couldn't pick up any other scents.

A countdown began, and I shook off all thoughts of what was in the water. With our luck, there was a valve that would release piranhas. At the sound of the horn, we pulled. My face twisted in pain as glass pierced my skin. Even with my shirt for protection, it felt like I dragged my palms across razors.

"Ahhh," Addie cried. Blood dripped down her forearm before splashing to the ground. Her thin shirt was of no use, and I fought back the elation her anguish caused me.

"Don't you fucking let go of the fucking rope, Addie," Conrad screamed. They moved closer to the pool's edge, losing ground each time Landry and I heaved the rope. It wouldn't be long before another person died.

She whined, fighting to keep her grip strong, but there was too much blood. Her hands kept slipping. "I'm tryin'. Stop yelling at me and pull."

Landry and I had a system by this point—a cadence . . . one . . . two . . . three . . . pull. Each round, we tugged Conrad and Addie closer to the pungent water.

Anger built in Addie's eyes, its fury directed toward me. If she could, she'd push me in and say fuck this game. Another reminder of just how fake our friendship was and another reason to miss Vi.

Determination set in, and on the next tug, I yanked so hard Addie slid just shy of the edge. Realizing they couldn't win and she'd go in, Addie let go of the rope and tried to move out of the way.

Landry and I landed in a heap as Conrad slipped, barreling for the water.

"What the fuck are you doing, you dumb bitch?" he shrieked, grabbing her ankle before he fell in. The liquid splashed, hitting Addie down the side of her face, and she screamed.

But my focus was on the bubbling liquid that ate through Conrad's flesh. Whatever was in the water methodically broke him down. This was far worse than watching Raymond burn.

What the fuck was in the pool? It damn sure wasn't water.

Conrad didn't even have a chance to cry out. I covered my mouth and looked on in shock as his skin separated from bone and the bone slowly dissolved. Clumps of fatty tissue turned to brown sludge as it floated to the water's surface.

"Drop the rope, Harper," Landry screamed, snapping me from my trance. I released my hold as he continued. "We don't know what's in there. I don't want you hurt."

"My face," Addie squealed. "It burns!"

I couldn't spare her a glance. I transfixed my gaze on the pool of acid and the fact that the only recognizable part left of Conrad was the hand sitting at the pool's edge.

Arms wrapped around me, wiping away tears I didn't know were falling. I turned my head into Landry's chest. "Why is this happening? Who would want to do this to us?" I muttered between sobs.

The sound of the door opening drew my attention. I needed to get out of here.

"Someone cheated death," Jack snickered. "I hope you know death never loses. Enjoy your temporary reprieve. Move to the next game."

It was Jim's laughter that chased us out of the space and into the adjacent room, but it was Jack's words that weighed heavily on me.

Death was coming for us all.

Erebus

G umbo grumbled impatiently at my feet, and I stroked along his skin while I watched the scene on the monitors unfold, laughing. I reached into the desk drawer and pulled out a bag of marshmallows, placing a few on the floor near the gator. They were his favorite snack, even if Minos disapproved of me feeding him sweets.

Most people didn't realize that gators were opportunistic feeders. They only needed to eat once a week. Sure, they ate things like fish, turtles, and snakes, but they wouldn't turn down potato chips, sausage, or the occasional human.

"You'll ruin his appetite," Minos muttered, and I flipped him off, my focus returning to the computer. He never wanted me, or Gumbo, to have any fun. Everything was too serious with him.

Adeline's acid burn was less than she deserved. Secretly, I had hoped that tug of war managed to take two of them out, but disfigurement would have to do since that didn't happen. Even if it was temporary. She wouldn't leave the house alive.

My attention moved back to my little nightmare. She was perfect, even with soot covering her cheek. A vision of heaven and hell wrapped in a pretty package. Her angry outburst earlier showed me a part of her she kept hidden from everyone around her.

Darkness swirled beneath the surface of her skin, and even though the walls of the house separated us, I could almost taste it. All night, I had been rooting for the thick thighed, raven-haired beauty, hoping she would make it. My dick had been harder than it had been in months. Seeing her crazy slowly inch its way out had me imagining her legs wrapped around my head while I plunged my tongue inside of her sweet pussy.

People said thick thighs saved lives, but they forgot how easily they could take them. I would gladly meet death while I suffocated between the silky flesh, my face covered in her arousal.

The next game was originally supposed to be a version of Four Square, but my heart lurched when I thought about Harper Leigh being forced to take part. With every bounce of the ball, the walls would slowly close in around them. I had attached knives to the panels to ensure that at least someone in the group bled out on the floor.

I didn't want that to happen, not until I had a turn with the woman I was staring at on the screen. If anyone was going to make her bleed, it would be me. The thought of her blood running down her skin, pooling between her breasts, made my cock throb, and I adjusted the way I was sitting, praying my brother wouldn't notice.

"Minos, I have to have her. She's meant for us. I know she is," I said as I stroked the bracelet on my wrist, thinking of one made of midnight black hair. I'd remove all the others if I could just have hers decorating my arm.

Minos closed his eyes and sighed deeply while rubbing at his temple. "Erebus, we've already discussed this. I'll consider it if she lives. The thing you need to be focused on is getting vengeance for Vi. You know what these bastards did to her."

Everything he said was the truth, but he forgot we could punish her in our own way. It seemed wasteful to discard someone like her. After we rectified her past behaviors, we could keep her. Surely, she would be easier to deal with than Gumbo when he was throwing a fit.

Minos had already caught me printing off a still of Harper. The last thing I wanted was for him to give me more shit about her. He didn't think she would make it out alive, but I fixated on just that. If she lived, she'd be mine. Ours.

When he turned his head, I pressed a button on my keyboard, shutting down the mechanism that controlled the walls in the next room before hitting play on the video. Harper hadn't figured out why they were stuck inside the house, which seemed strange. From everything Vi had said about her and the way she played our games, she was too intelligent not to have pieced together the puzzle placed before her.

Evening had settled outside, painting the sky in black and deep indigos. Lightning bugs flew through the sky, the green lights flickering intermittently. The group of friends that had once gathered outside had mostly disbanded, choosing to hide indoors, away from the swarms of mosquitoes that plagued Louisiana's southern evenings. Over the video, the heavy bass from the music drifted in the air, adding to the symphony of insects.

Two of the men stood by a patio table. They spoke in low tones, and from the quality of the feed, it was difficult to decipher exactly what they had said. One pulled something from his pocket and deposited it into the cups the other was holding. Afterward, he opened the back door and ushered his companion in, both vanishing from sight.

Harper turned to her boyfriend and the other female while crossing her arms over her chest. "What did Ray and Conrad put in those cups?" she demanded, her voice edged with anger. Even over the monitor, I could feel animosity rolling off her in waves.

Landry lowered his voice and attempted to placate her by touching her shoulder. "Babe, I'm sure it was nothing. You know how they were."

Harper shoved his hand away and glared in his direction. "Exactly. I know how they were. Quit playing dumb." She seemed like she was one second away from completely losing it on him, and I grabbed a marshmallow from the bag, waiting to see what happened next.

Landry gripped his hair and pulled. "I don't know what you want me to say, Harper Leigh. I can't ask either of them now because they're dead. This is ridiculous. I just lost my two best friends, and you're giving me shit over what? We don't even know who drank those drinks. Maybe they did."

I narrowed my eyes at the monitor and decided I didn't really want to know what would happen next. Over the system, I spoke calmly. "Now, now, children. As much as I'm enjoying this lover's spat, I need you to proceed to the next room. You'll enjoy the game we have planned."

Harper was the only one who would enjoy anything, but she didn't know it yet. I couldn't wait to see the look on her face. The remaining three players took hesitant steps into the space where blades covered the walls. I had to act normal, so I didn't draw attention to myself. "The game that we're going to play is four square. Hopefully, everyone is familiar with the rules."

"There aren't four of us anymore," Harper shrieked at me. My dick hardened at her defiance. It was something that I would have to fuck out of her, yet another thing to punish.

I smiled to myself. "Well, you'll have to improvise. Every bounce of the ball brings with it an extra special surprise."

I typed on the keyboard in front of me, acting like it was business as usual, even if it was anything but. Feeling extra jovial, I hit play, letting music bleed over the speakers. Harper scoffed, and my smile widened. She had no idea what was in store for her.

"Clock's ticking," I stated, sitting back in my chair. My little nightmare picked up the ball and bounced it across the painted lines on the floor to Addie. I let it go on for a few moments and said nothing.

Suddenly, Harper caught the ball and turned, looking directly at the camera. It was almost as if she knew exactly where it was. "This game is boring," she mocked. "Surely, you and Jack can do better than this."

She'd given us nicknames. My heart fluttered in my chest at the fact she thought so much of us. Slowly, I stood and leaned into the mic. "Minos, we have a slight technical difficulty. We need to improvise. Grab Charon and Thanatos. It's time to have a little fun." He grunted at me as his fingers flew over his phone.

I grabbed my mask, securing it so that none of my face was showing. Harper hadn't earned the right to see what I truly looked like. "Don't kill them. Not yet, at least." I stalked to the door and stopped. "And Harper? She's mine."

He probably thought it was so I could teach her a lesson for mocking us, but that was the furthest thing from my mind. I needed her more than oxygen, just one taste. She would learn something tonight. The first thing was that her body belonged to me.

Harper Leigh

The temperature in the room dropped as three men walked inside. Each was dressed in black from head to toe. They were tall with broad shoulders, and wore Venetian masks that hid the features of their face, a mockery of the Mardi Gras tradition. Until right then, I hadn't realized that there were more than two of them. Jim and Jack had been more than enough to contend with. Now I would have to devise a name for the third man. Without hearing their voices, I couldn't tell who was who. All I knew was that their appearance meant trouble for me. *I needed to learn to keep my mouth shut.*

The first one leaned against the wall, completely at ease with the situation. A hammer decorated the mask, and a chill ran along my skin, causing goosebumps to form. He hooked his fingers and beckoned for Addie to come with him. "You." His deep voice was unfamiliar. Johnny. That was what I would call him until I could escape. Addie clutched at Landry, probably hoping to save herself. My boyfriend, well ex, if we made it out of the house alive, tucked an arm around her to shield her from the man's sight.

I rolled my eyes at the gesture. *Of course, now he wants to play the hero.* I approached Addie and shoved her toward the man who requested her presence. Her eyes widened as she stumbled into Johnny, and Landry stared at me. "What the fuck, Harper?"

I took a deep breath and clenched my jaw. "We might as well get this over with. It's not like either of us can save her."

Addie screamed and thrashed as Johnny picked her up. Dark laughter echoed off the walls as her legs flailed mid-air. They disappeared through the door, leaving us with who I assumed were Jim and Jack.

Landry was next. The man with a bleeding butterfly decorating his mask stalked forward, and my heart caught in my throat. He was intimidating, and I waited for him to speak, curious which one of our captors he was. His footsteps reverberated in the room, and he grabbed Landry's hair, jerking him. My boyfriend was an idiot and fell to his knees, fear consuming him. If he thought dead weight would stop them, he was wrong.

Masked man number two simply turned on his heel and dragged Landry across the floor. I heard a sob escape from his mouth, and I pursed my lips. Adrenaline and fear had consumed me since entering Toussaint Manor, but I wouldn't cower in front of the men who thought they had trapped me. Even if fight or flight told me to fight, there was no way I could overpower the wraith in the corner.

I lifted my chin toward the shadow, waiting to see what he would do. Slowly, he sauntered forward, like he didn't have a care in the world. Like molasses in winter, my mama would have said. A crow decorated his mask, its wings spread over his cheeks. Another shudder ran across my body.

His demeanor differed from the other two men, and the air rushed from my lungs when he spoke. "Cher, I see you aren't afraid like your friends. Why is that?"

The timbre of his voice was like silk, and I reminded myself to square my shoulders while I thought about his question. Not that I was fearless, but I was resigned. Some things didn't make sense to me anymore. "If you're going to kill me, there is nothing I can do to stop you." I hesitated momentarily, unsure of how much honesty I should convey. "Plus, I don't know who to trust anymore."

He held out his hand, and I grabbed it, holding on to it like a lifeline. "I've got an *envie* to have some fun. Care to join me?"

My brain screamed at me to say no or run, but I stepped forward with him instead. "*Allons*." We left behind the room with knives on the walls and entered a dark corridor.

Outside, the weather was getting worse. I hadn't been paying attention as we dodged fireballs or when the people I had once called my friends had been dying. Despite being led down a dim hallway, I could hear the rain battering the roof, and the wind howled like a *rougarou*. Limbs thrashed, beating against the side of the house while thunder shook its foundation.

A door creaked open at the end of the long hallway, and Jim tugged me inside. Along the walls, candles flickered, their wax dripping down the sides. A hook dangled from the ceiling, and I wondered why here. What was so special about this room? What would he do to me?

Slowly, Jim turned, and he brushed his fingers across the palm of my hand in an odd show of reassurance. I noticed the top of them was covered in tattoos that disappeared beneath the sleeves of his shirt. Braided bracelets made of hair decorated his wrists, and I swallowed, unsure of what to think. "Do you trust me, Harper Leigh?"

The sound of my name on his lips made my blood warm rather than cool. My body was simply confused by the excessive adrenaline and horror of the evening. I shook my head, trying to clear my thoughts. "Not even a little, Jim."

He chuckled at me before encasing my wrists in his hand. "Good," he murmured, securing them with a thick zip tie. "It's more fun that way."

Screams filled the empty space of the house, the sound louder than the storm raging outside. My captor abruptly jerked my arms over my head and lifted me, securing me to the hook I had observed earlier. The position stretched my body and forced me onto my toes.

"Erebus," he murmured as his thumb traced my bottom lip. Without another word, he moved behind me, his fingertips gliding down my spine.

"What?" I managed to choke out. Until I felt his hands on my skin, I had accomplished staying calm. Once he touched me, panic welled back up in the pit of my stomach, swirling there. It threatened to suffocate me as my heart pounded in my ears, muffling out the screams that could only belong to Landry.

He clicked his tongue as if he knew what I was thinking. "You can call me Erebus, little nightmare. I love that you already came up with a nickname for me. Perhaps one day I'll tell you my real name, but first, you have to earn it."

His hand traveled further south, cupping my ass and squeezing tightly. "No," I whined, kicking backward and hoping to make impact. His touches confused me, causing fire to erupt beneath my flesh.

He grunted when I landed a kick and wrapped his arms around my waist as he rested his head on my shoulder. "That's it. I like it when you hurt me."

Leisurely, he trailed a hand down my torso as I struggled against him, my thoughts warring with one another. The logical part of my brain begged him to stop, but my body had other plans. Erebus yanked the front of my jeans up, forcing the seam of them to rub against my clit. Sparks flew through my veins at the sensation. Landry had never touched me like that. The most we'd ever done was kiss.

I whimpered and jerked against my restraints. "Let me go. You don't have to do this," I told him as he caressed along the seam of my jeans. Shame heated my cheeks because I was enjoying the sensations he caused. At any moment, dampness would seep through the denim, and he would know my secret.

What made everything worse was that I hadn't even allowed my boyfriend to touch me like that. Now, a stranger was. One that I couldn't see their face and didn't know their name.

"Why would I stop, Harper? I know that you're enjoying our little game. If I were to slide my fingers inside of you right now, how wet would you be? How tightly would your pussy grip my hand?" he crooned. He rubbed faster, and I almost wanted to beg him to continue. Something was happening between my legs and inside my body that I had never experienced before. I pressed my thighs together, hoping to ease the ache forming.

Without warning, he stopped, and I cried out from . . . frustration? Relief? After tonight, if I lived, me and my body were going to have a long talk. Erebus shifted behind me, and something smooth, cold, and metallic stroked along my exposed skin at the small of my back. I attempted to figure out what it was.

Addie's screams joined Landry's in a symphony of horror, and I shivered. "Don't worry," Erebus whispered in my ear. "What I have planned for you is substantially better than what your friends are experiencing."

His free hand snaked along my torso as the metal continued to kiss my skin. It wasn't sharp like a knife, instead rounded. He ripped the cup of my bra down, and my nipples hardened in the air. Suddenly, he was in front of me, and I could see what he was doing. In his hand sat a gun. I fought to push down the scream that bubbled up in my throat at the sight as I watched in fascination.

Erebus's motions were unrushed and gentle as he swirled the tip of the weapon around my nipple until it was a tight peak that throbbed. "Please let me go," I tried to plead one last time before the tidal wave inside of me pulled me under, taking with it any bit of sanity that was remaining.

He tilted his head at my words, the crow painted on the mask mocking me. "Mmm." The gun moved to my other breast, and he continued the motion while the opposite hand pinched at my already sensitive nipple, causing me to hiss. "I. Don't. Think. So. Do you know why I call you little nightmare?"

I didn't respond, sure that he would tell me. "I call you that because I can see this glimmer of darkness beneath your skin, begging to be set free. My brother doesn't agree with me, but I want to keep you. It's okay, though. I'm very convincing when I need to be."

Erebus released my nipple, and I tried to ignore how they throbbed, pleading to be touched. The cold steel traveled down along my ribs, and I was aware that, at that moment, I was in more danger than I had been all evening, which was saying something. The masked man held my life in his hands. Despite that, I watched him touch me, stopping only long enough to unbutton my pants and jerk them with my panties down my thighs.

If I could use my hands, I would have attempted to cover myself from the gaze of Erebus. It completely exposed me to him and the cold air. I was at his mercy, and unable to do anything to stop him. My muscles shook from not only fatigue and the chill, but also the adrenaline that had made a reappearance. My stomach flipped as the gun continued its descent.

A strangled sound fell from my mouth as the pistol glided along my mons and slipped between my folds. If I didn't die from being shot or tortured, I would from embarrassment at the noises I was trying to suppress. Erebus took his time rubbing the metal over a sensitive spot no one had ever touched but me. "I would have cut off your clothes if it were up to me. Made you parade around the house in nothing so my brothers could see your pretty pussy and tits. I couldn't do that, though. Not unless I carved out your boyfriend's eyes. I don't want him ever looking at you again."

Sometimes late at night, when no one was around, I would let my fingers brush against my clit, but I had only ever ended up more frustrated than before. Every pass of the steel and filthy word the masked man spoke caused the wildfire inside me to burn hotter and brighter.

"Do you like that, little nightmare?" Erebus murmured, his voice almost mocking me. "Do you let Landry touch you like this? Maybe I should cut off his fingers in front of you. Let him watch me as I fuck you."

Without warning, the cold steel pushed inside of me in one brutal shove. Pain shot through me as it moved in and out, and a garbled noise caught in my throat. It was brutal. Savage. And it caused the most exquisite feeling I had ever known to race through my body. With every thrust, the pain morphed into something else entirely, leaving nothing but a sensation of fullness and pleasure.

The gun grazed against a spot deep inside of me I hadn't known existed, and I squeezed my eyes shut, focusing on that. "Look at me, little nightmare. I want you to see me while you come," Erebus commanded.

My eyes flickered open as fireworks exploded within me. The edges of my vision darkened as I shuddered against my restraints, and liquid warmth ran down my thighs. To my further embarrassment, Erebus kneeled down and ran his fingers through the arousal pooled on my skin. "You didn't tell me you were a virgin, Harper," he growled, sniffing at my flesh.

He tugged my ballet flats off and pulled my pants the rest of the way off. I was too caught up in the aftereffects of the orgasm to argue with him. The bliss was almost enough to sedate me. "Well, you didn't ask. Would you have given me a choice?"

The sound of his pants unzipping caught my attention, and I glanced at his hand. Unceremoniously, the gun clattered to the floor as he pulled his cock out. It was angry and hard. A metal piercing glinted in the candlelight. And it was large. There was no way it would fit inside of me. "No," I told him, trying to keep my voice steady.

His palm traveled along his length, stroking it, and he reached for one of my thighs. "Yes," he told me as he positioned the head at my already sore entrance. "I would have never let a gun take your virginity, little nightmare. I want your blood coating my cock while your pussy drenches me."

He gave me no warning as he impaled me on his shaft, his hips snapping against mine. His fingers dug into the flesh of my leg as he hooked it around his waist. "I could have made it good for you, cher, but this is all we have," he murmured as he pistoned in and out of me. Every stroke pressed my nipples against his shirt and provided friction to my clit.

My body was no longer my own, and I let go. I allowed my hips to move with his, too caught up in the intensity of every thrust. The words from my mouth were nothing more than a chant drowning out the screams and the thunder. Bruises would form on my skin, but that was the least of my problems.

I itched to touch him. Let my nails dig into the skin of his back. Take off his mask and see who exactly was beneath it.

My pussy clenched around him, and he groaned, ramming into me harder. "You like this, little nightmare? You want me to treat you like my good little slut? Fill you with my cum and mark you as my own?"

I closed my eyes and let my head fall back when everything became too much. Erebus began to pant and pump faster, his body slapping against mine as a second climax approached. "You have to pull out," I begged, my voice lost in the chaos.

"Never. I promise that if you live through tonight, I intend to fill you up every day." My eyes stung at his words. The last thing that should have been on my mind was birth control, but I wasn't on any. If he came inside of me, I could get pregnant—if I lived.

"But–"

He cut me off by placing the palm of his hand over my mouth. "The only place I am going to come from now on is inside this tight little pussy."

A tear trickled down my face even as my body shook against him and my walls wrapped around him like a vise. More warmth ran down my thighs as his cock twitched inside of me. He buried his face into my neck, and his fingers brushed through my hair. "Shh. Don't cry, Harper. It could be worse. You weren't crushed by a wall or burned alive."

His words rang true, but they didn't stop the pain radiating between my legs. Or the shame running through my head. I'd lost my virginity to someone I didn't know. Was it considered cheating if I had no choice? Did any of that matter?

Like nothing had happened, he pulled away from me and took out his phone. The flash went off as he took a picture of me trussed up. And then one of his cock. True to his word, it was coated in my blood. He tucked his dick back in his pants. Then he untethered my arms, snapping the tie holding my wrists. "Get dressed. We have another game to play."

My cheeks flamed further from his words as I readjusted my bra. Despite the ache in my legs and the tremble of my muscles, I shrugged on my pants as fast as possible.

The entire time, he stood near the door, his arms crossed over his chest like he hadn't completely turned my world upside down.

MINOS

I fisted my cock, pumping to match the tempo Erebus fucked the black widow. The image of what her virgin blood on the gun must have looked like made me rock hard—another reason she needed to go.

I'd been so fixated on Erebus and Harper that I missed Thanatos' and Charon's handy work. Not even the shrieks from Addie as Charon used some tiger claw contraption to rake down her tits as she rode him were enough to draw my attention. She thought it would save her, but she wasn't enough of a pull. I snorted when I thought how terrible of a lay the Ken doll had to be if both his girls came all over two of my brothers' cocks.

Thanatos had other plans for Landry. His screams were so loud I thought we'd be discovered even out in the bayou. Luckily, he passed out from the pain. None of what happened in those rooms held my focus. My focus was on the sounds Harper made.

My hand jerked in tandem as Erebus thrust so violently inside her that Harper screamed. The sound sent a jolt down the base of my spine. "Fuck," I shouted as I slid my fist up my shaft, rubbing my thumb over the pierced head. The two barbells heightened my need to come. So I doubled my speed, squeezing my length as Harper's moans burst through the speakers.

I whipped my head toward the screen. Tears streamed down her face, emphasizing her full pouty lips, swollen from her arousal. She was a goddamn vision—her head thrown back, turmoil written all over her features as fear and lust battled for supremacy.

Harper's hips matched Erebus's pace, and I jerked myself even harder. My cock pulsed, signaling my impending orgasm. Erebus groaned, telling me how perfectly her walls wrapped around him, and I snapped my eyes closed. Visions of the feel of her tight, wet pussy clamping down so hard it bruised my shaft played through my mind. My cock stiffened at the thought, and my balls drew tight.

"Fuck . . . fuck . . . fuuckk," I snarled. All the blood rushed from my brain to my dick. Ropes of my cum shot in bursts across the monitor, landing almost perfectly over Harper's face. I moaned, pumping every last drop from my semi-erect cock in time to hear her beg for Erebus not to come in her.

My gaze focused on the screen as the dumb fucker released inside her.

"Enjoying yourself, brother?" Erebus asked, jolting me from the high of my release.

I swiveled in my seat to face him as I shoved my dick back into my black denim jeans. Not bothering to clean myself or the monitors. "How long have you been standing there like an idiot?"

"Long enough to see you rub one out." He smirked, licking Harper's blood off his fingers.

"How does she taste?" I questioned, gritting my teeth for even caring. Yet another strike against her.

Harper Leigh helped kill our sister, and for that, she'd die with the rest of the stupid shits here tonight. My dick hardened. What was coming next was my second favorite game of the night. If Harper somehow survived what was to come, she wouldn't during the last trial.

"Like ours. She's sin and innocence—we just have to find the key to unlock her darkness."

Clenching my jaw, I glared at him. "You can't keep her, Erebus. She killed Vi, and for that, she'll die just like the others. Our sister's soul is roaming. We need to make this right, or Vi will put the gris-gris on us."

He knew better than to play with the spirits. We came here with one intention—giving them the end they deserved.

"How many times did you replay this before I came back upstairs?"

"It's time for the next video," I grumbled, ignoring his question. He was only goading me.

Erebus laughed, and Pollo and Arty growled at him. "Play nice, or Gumbo will get a late-night snack."

Undeterred by his threats, they both snarled, exposing their canines. I made a mental note to give them steak once we returned home.

I spun and faced the computer, waiting for Harper to enter the room where her sleazy boyfriend and whoring best friend were.

There were only three of them left. Addie tucked herself into Landry's side; both of them looked worse for wear. The open gashes on the side of Landry's face were cut nearly to the bone before Thanatos cauterized the wound. Couldn't have him bleed out before his time. Addie was stripped down to her panties, and angry red claw marks marred her tits. I had hoped there would be more damage, making her outside match her inside.

As soon as Harper walked into the room, her eyes narrowed in on where they were joined. Landry pushed from Addie's side. "What did they do to you?" he asked, taking in her disheveled state.

"What happened to you?" Harper croaked.

Enough of this shit. I hit play on the video. My anger renewed as Vi stumbled out of the house. Her movements were so sluggish. She made her way down to the pier, and I kept hoping for another outcome, knowing it would never happen. I closed my eyes, not wanting to see her fall, only for a shrill cry to force them back open.

"No," Harper screamed in shocked horror. Her hand flew to her mouth, and she fell to the ground as Vi struggled before her body went limp.

Landry bent to help her. "Come on, Harp. Get up."

"Get the fuck away from me," Harper hissed.

Scrunching my brows, I turned to Erebus. "What the hell is that about? Why is she acting surprised?"

HARPER LEIGH

"*H*oly shit! I think she's dead. Try harder," *Landry barked.*

She was missing. She couldn't be dead.

"*No… no… no. This can't be happening!*" *Conrad exclaimed.*

"What did you do? What the fuck was in those cups, Landry?" I screamed from my spot on the floor. I couldn't hold myself up. My knees buckled when I saw Vi stumble down toward the dock. I kept willing her to stop—to fall in the grass. Anything that prevented the horrifying scene.

"I can't find a pulse. We've been at this for ten minutes. We need to call the police," Adeline shrieked.

My gaze flew to the screen. They got her out of the lake. Maybe there was a chance she survived.

"Are you out of your fucking mind? Did you forget my dad's the mayor, up for reelection this year? We can't afford to kill Hades's daughter."

Things were coming together. What they did. It's why we were here.

"I can explain," Landry began, but I silenced him with a glare.

Standing, I refocused on the video clip.

"Let's dump her back in the lake. The gators will get her, and we can deal with her car tomorrow. You're fucking lucky you kicked everyone out when you did," Adeline stated. "Or there's no way you'd be able to cover up that you drugged her."

My mind worked to process what I was witnessing. Addie was a bitch on the best of days, but suggesting murder? I waited for the echoes of nos, the pushes to call for help, or we shouldn'ts. None of that came.

"We can't hope the gators get her. What if they don't?" Landry whined.

Murderers. They were all fucking murderers. Addie instructed Raymond, and like the good little pup he was, he ran to do her bidding. Minutes later, he returned with a pack of chicken. They really were going to kill her.

"There's one now. I told you the raw meat would work. I'm surprised one didn't snatch her when she first splashed into the water."

I whirled around at a half-naked Addie. I expected to find remorse. Instead, she smiled, proud of herself. "Someone had to take initiative—"

"Shut the fuck up, Addie," Landry growled before he attempted to reach out for me. "Listen. I just . . . just let me explain."

Whatever he was going to say was cut off by a high-pitched wail.

"Fuck, she wasn't dead!"

My stomach roiled, and I twisted and bent over, throwing up. The sound of my best friend's cries as an alligator ate her alive seared my brain. It would live in my memories for eternity.

Before I could react, Jack's voice came over the speakers. "Now you know why you're all here. You've all been tried and found guilty. Take solace from the fact you get to die together." The door to this room opened before he continued. "It's the only kindness you'll get."

Addie ran out of the room with her proverbial tail between her legs. *The stupid cunt.* Her smugness disappeared faster than Mawmaw's beignets. However, Landry looked at me, pleading with his eyes. *Fuck him too! If we find a way out of this, I'm going to castrate the fucker and make him eat his own dick.* I stormed past him. He'd need to beg his maker because that was the only person who'd offer him forgiveness.

I entered what looked like another area for hosting a gathering. Smaller than the ballroom we were in earlier, but larger than a living room or game room. The red walls had holes in them, exposing the insulation, and layers of dust covered what little furniture was in the space. A further sign of the mansion's dilapidated state. Much like the first room, this one also had a checkered floor.

Landry stopped at my side. "Baby, let me explain." If he were smart, he'd go over to where his *girlfriend* was.

"I'm not interested in any of your or Addie's explanations," I seethed.

Growling, Landry gripped my arm so hard I winced. "You'll let me explain, Harper Leigh. That's what good Christian girlfriends do. What would your daddy think of this behavior?"

I wanted to laugh at him. Good Christian girlfriend? I was very familiar with how Christian girlfriends behaved. He had me fucked up if he thought I'd roll over and take it. My hand flew up, striking him in his throat. His arm dropped, and I moved out of his reach. "Well, he's not here to share his opinion on the matter, is he?" I scowled, reveling in the redness of his face as he gasped for breath, massaging his throat. Over this bullshit night, I surveyed the room, looking for where the damn cameras were. Huffing, I shouted, "Can we get this shit moving already?"

It didn't take long for instructions to come through the speakers. Jim spoke this time. Another fucked up version of a recess game. Red Light, Green Light. We had to run on green and stop on red. The goal: don't land on a booby-trapped tile. The game would last until at least one person died.

"*Bon chance* and *laissez les bons temps rouler,*" Jim cackled before the countdown sounded as the floor lit up.

Why the hell was the floor illuminated? The question became a fleeting thought when an actual traffic light lowered and flashed green. I darted across the floor, praying to get to the other side before it turned red.

"Red light," a computerized voice stated.

I halted on a black-tiled square, waiting for something to happen. Moments passed before Jim bellowed. "You have all survived the first round." Squares darkened around me. That's when I noticed how close to me Landry and Addie were. "Stop on any unlit tile and suffer the consequences," Jim explained.

I groaned. Of course, there was more to this game. Why would they make it simple?

"Green light."

I barely made it two steps before 'red light' was called. Jim offered another mocking congratulation before three more lit tiles went dark. Then the traffic light flashed, and I took off.

"Red light."

I internally cursed, nearly toppling over. The pulse in my throat thrummed like the drums of war.

"When we make it out of this, you and I are going to have a serious talk," Landry hissed, alerting me to his closeness.

It was a pity I couldn't hit him again.

"I don't know why you bother with her, Landry. Harper obviously doesn't understand what it takes to remain on top," Addie alleged.

Flexing his jaw, Landry twisted toward her. "Will you just be quiet?" he demanded.

She huffed, but did as she was ordered.

I rolled my eyes. "You don't need to silence her. She's right. I don't know if–"

"Green light."

A whooshing noise echoed in the room. My head jerked in the direction of the sound in time to duck before the axe flew through the air and whizzed by. "Shit," Landry grunted, squatting. He narrowly escaped being hit.

How unfortunate.

The idea of his death happening via being impaled had a certain je ne sais quoi to it.

"Oh, did we forget to mention each round, you'll also have to dodge whatever weapons fly through the air?" Jack jested.

I hopped to another tile as a spear sailed across the room, wishing one of them would just die already.

"This is ridiculous," Addie screeched. "You can't do this! It isn't fair." She stomped her foot.

Rage boiled in my veins as I jumped to a white square to her left. "Right, because what y'all did to Vi was so fair?" I muttered.

"Red light."

We all froze. I swiveled my head, observing their proximity to me. Addie was just ahead of me, and Landry was four tiles away but in the same row. We were more than halfway across the room. The door out of here couldn't be more than eight or nine steps from where I stood.

Shaking out my limbs, I bounced on the balls of my feet and prepared to run.

"Green light."

I dashed forward, mindful of my surroundings, but slowed when throwing stars whipped in batches of fours from both walls.

"Son of a bitch," Landry yelped.

Pausing, I peered to my left. He had a star sticking out of his side. Hello karma, is that you? Sadly, the wound wasn't life-threatening. A few stitches, and he'd be fine.

"Red light."

"Landry," Addie squealed.

She was directly in front of me, focused on Landry, just as three spiked clubs launched. I waited, gauging their speed before shoving Addie.

"What the f–?" Addie screeched. Her words cut off when a club smashed into the side of her skull, covering me in mushed goo before I could move out of the way. She blinked a few times, like her brain hadn't registered what happened. Seconds later, she crumpled to the ground. Sections of her face were strewn around her head.

Lifting my hands, I scooped the clumps of Addie's brain and chipped bone off me. "Fucking gross," I groaned, flicking my fingers free of the muck. "I misjudged the velocity," I muttered.

"Harper Leigh. Why would you push her?" Landry yelled, gawking at his now-dead fun toy.

I ignored his righteous outrage, more interested in Addie's prone form and the macabre scene in front of me. The whole side of her face was sunken in, clear past her skull. The back of her head was cracked open, and chunks of grayish-pink matter oozed down a spike before it landed near the remainder of her cheek. Her one remaining eye was forever frozen in shock as her blood seeped out onto the white tile she lay on. I stepped around her, staring in fascination at the portion of her jaw resting on the floor. Leaning over her, I counted the teeth that scattered like shards of broken glass. *Eleven.*

"Please proceed to the next game," Jack ordered as the door opened.

I strode halfway toward the exit before turning to take one last look at Addie. A smile appeared on my face, and I laughed.

"What's so funny?" Landry asked from the doorway.

Spinning back to face him, I retorted, "I guess karma just needed a little push." Landry's eyebrows reached his hairline, and my laugh turned into a cackle. I shrugged my shoulders and walked past him. He always had a terrible sense of humor.

EREBUS

My little nightmare had survived yet again. The previous trial had been the most difficult one yet. Red Light, Green Light with knives and axes? It had been a pure stroke of genius when we had brainstormed that one.

A pang of sadness hit me, and I stroked along the bracelets lining my wrist. Harper Leigh probably wouldn't survive the next game. It was a shame because I wanted to keep her. One evening with her wasn't enough.

She was confusing, though. Her reaction to Viola's death puzzled me. She was there, and her vitriolic speech to Landry and Addie made little sense, especially the fact that she never wanted to see them again. Was she playing us? Trying to muddle the truth?

Despite her role in Vi's death, I still desired to keep her. Cage her and lock her away forever, so no one else could ever see her again. I could teach her to behave and abide by my rules. After all, I had done that exact thing with Gumbo.

Absentmindedly, I reached down and caressed the gator at my feet, who let out a little grunt. "Minos, let's keep her," I pleaded to my brother, who stared at the monitors, poking out my bottom lip for good measure. I knew he was as affected by her as I was.

He sat back in his chair and rubbed his eyes, done with the conversation. "Fine. Only if she lives through the remaining games. All of them," he said with a sigh, not looking at the pouty face I made.

Victory had never felt as sweet. I did a fist pump in the air and said a silent prayer to Monsieur Agoussou that he would protect Harper. I was so close to having her as mine.

My finger hovered over a button on the keyboard, and I stalled, my mind racing. I wondered what Harper would think when she saw the next video clip. What would her reaction be to the events that unfolded before her? Sure, she knew about Viola's death, but there was no way she knew what happened afterward.

Grinning to myself, I hit the key and sat back in my chair, waiting for chaos to erupt.

It was pitch black, and the sound of the frogs filled the background with a symphony of noise. The moon shined down on the lake's surface, reflecting back a silvery glow. If you stared closely at the screen, you could see bodies tangled with one another on the ground near the water's edge.

"Fuck, just like that, Landry. Don't stop," a feminine voice moaned.

"You're going to take this dick like the good slut you are. Your pussy feels so good. I can't believe I waited this long to fuck you," Landry grunted.

Even in the shadows of the night, slivers of skin were evident. Traces of a leg or arm. Whimpers and groans filled the air, drowning out everything else.

"Don't pull out, please," the woman whined.

"That's right, going to fill this sweet cunt up."

After several moments, everything went quiet. "Tell me you'll leave Harper, the Bible thumper. You know she'll never put out."

I smirked to myself, remembering what we had done and the blood running down her thighs. Nothing pleased me more than knowing I was the only one who had touched her. I was her first.

"Addie, get it out of your head that we're going to be together. You're just an easy lay. Harper is the kind of girl you marry."

The sound of a slap echoed in the night. "The kind of girl that lays there like a dead fish once a week. Even if you marry her, you'll never get enough of me. Admit it, Landry. Harper is just safe and easy. She's gullible and believes all of the shit you tell her. Wonder if she knows that last week you ate me out on her bed?"

"Shut the fuck up. I'll kill you if you ever tell her. Fuck up my plans and you'll end up in the lake with Vi."

HARPER LEIGH

"Wonder if she still thinks I'm safe and easy?" I turned toward Landry. Then I lifted my finger, pretending to mull it over before I continued. "Oh, wait. She can't think with half her head caved in," I singsonged, even more thrilled with my decision to push the skank. Vi was right, Addie was no good, and Landry was scum.

I'd probably be more devastated if he didn't kill my best friend. I'd noticed the sneaky touches and lingering glances all night. My mind was made up to end things with him before I saw the video.

"Baby," Landry tried. He'd been weary of me since I pushed Addie. *I guess he's not as dumb as he looks.*

Narrowing my eyes, I glared at him. "Don't tell me. You want me to let you explain? Am I right?"

"Harper. It was nothing. She meant nothing to me," Landry explained. Too bad I gave less than zero fucks.

"On to the next game," Jack commanded.

I sighed, storming through the door. Perhaps I'd get lucky, and there'd be a gator this scum could be fed to.

Landry ran up next to me, keeping pace. "Harper, please, baby. Let me fix this," he begged as we entered another part of the mansion. This one had paisley print wallpaper, high vaulted ceilings, and a fireplace that had seen better days. A stainless steel table was among the sparse furniture, its obvious newness making it stand out.

"Move, you murderous, cheating son of a bitch," I snapped, shoving his chest.

"You shouldn't throw stones if you live in a glass house, Harper. You literally just killed someone. We're even. We can escape from here together and then work this out," he suggested.

It was my turn to be shocked. I gawped at his audacity. *Stupid idiot has never faced a real consequence in his over-privileged life.* If Landry somehow made it out of here, his daddy would erase it all. "Get the hell outta my way, Landry Nicklaus Boutin!"

"Enough!" Jack barked over the intercom. "It's time to begin the next game. One of you won't make it out of this room, so your lover's spat is meaningless."

Growling, Landry spun around and stalked further into the room. "This isn't over, Harper. You're mine. I put too much work into this, and you won't leave me," he spat over his shoulder.

My lip curled in disgust as my anger mounted. I knew his words were true. Our parents planned to announce our engagement after Christmas. I didn't have any objections until tonight.

We passed a table lined with weapons. Scalpels, a bone saw, a mallet of some sort, a machete, garrote, knives, and so much more. What the hell childhood game were we perverting now? My fingers wrapped around the mallet, weighing it in my palm. I admired the shine of the tool orthopedic surgeons used to chip at bone.

"When you get home, I'll fuck your throat hoarse, pop that cherry, and put a baby in you. It would be in your best interest to stop fucking with me, Harper. I've only ever shown my nice guy side. You don't want me to introduce you to the guy that fucked Addie," Landry rambled.

I remained silent, pretending to be listening as we neared the exam-like table. Oblivious, he prattled on about all the shit I would and wouldn't do, and the consequences I would endure if I didn't comply. A whooshing sound thumped in my ears as my hand rose and my arm reared back. I swung two consecutive blows with the full force of my body weight to the back of his head before he registered what I'd done. Landry dropped to the floor, knocked out cold. A small patch of blood stained his hair. Gazing down, I noticed the pieces of skin mixed in with strands of hair.

"You finally shut the fuck up," I exclaimed, massaging the bridge of my nose. Dropping the mallet, I bent over, slid my arms under his armpits, and tugged him near the table, leaving a trail of blood in our wake. "Fuck, I forgot how heavy you are," I mumbled, thankful for the times I'd pulled his drunken ass to his room.

Huffing, I caught my breath and stared down at Landry's prone body, lying strewn on the steel surface. It took me what felt like hours to lift him onto the exam table. I needed to hurry. He still hadn't so much as twitched, but I couldn't stall any longer. I stalked over to the area we passed entering and grabbed the machete and the scalpel.

It was oddly silent as I stood over Landry. They announced no instructions for the game. No orders to stop came. It was just me and my thoughts. The day of the party by the lake and the video clips of what happened when I left played on a loop.

Con handed us the two solo cups. I missed the signs that night. He hovered, waiting to see us drink, but my phone went off, and I left. If I knew Vi, she drank both cups of the spiked drink. It was fitting he died being liquified. He was the reason she fell into the lake.

My ex was handsome, even with the burn on his face. Maybe if he had been less attractive, he'd have an ounce of humility. I doubted it, though. Landry had access to money. Looks helped, but money meant power, and power made people stupidly bold sometimes.

Vi's sluggish movements before she stilled in the water. Alone . . . she was alone.

Pain ripped through my chest. "I should've been there for you, Vi," I whispered. Guilt seeped through my pores, permeating the surrounding air with its toxicity. I bit the inside of my cheek until a metallic taste hit my tongue and fought back the tears. I'd fix this.

Her body lay still. They made a piss poor attempt to revive her. Only checking her pulse. No one called the police, too fearful of ruining Landry's father's mayoral re-election campaign.

I hummed *Iko Iko* as I cut his jeans and boxer briefs next, leaving him exposed. I stared at his erection. "You get off on pain?" I mumbled. "How fitting."

Raymond as he ran out of the house with the chicken to draw the gators. He'd sealed his fate. He was barbecued like the raw meat he had fetched. "Stupid fucker. I should've roasted marshmallows as you charred," I murmured.

Turning, I picked up the scalpel. The coolness of it was a stark contrast to my over-heated skin. I pressed the sharp point against the left side of Landry's neck just enough for a trickle of red to appear. Goosebumps lined my neck, and my nipples hardened. "Guess I get off on inflicting pain." My shoulders slumped. This would be more fun if he were awake.

Addie, as she heartlessly gloated like a proud peacock when her idea to draw the gators that ate my best friend alive worked. "Pride goeth before the fall, you cunt," I snapped. My only regret was not seeing her face when she realized I pushed her.

That left one person to serve penance—Landry. I understood why we were here. This couldn't end until Vi received retribution. My ex may not have been the catalyst or the person who suggested how to get rid of Vi's body, but he was complicit. A willing and eager accomplice. "You whined like a baby-back bitch about your daddy," I seethed as I sliced through his carotid artery until I nicked bone like butter. Crimson fluids poured down his throat as his eyes popped open. Landry peered up at me before he shot up into a sitting position. I could only imagine the adrenaline that was coursing through his veins. The fight or flight that misfired, encouraging him to act. His hands flew to his throat, but it was too late. He opened his mouth to speak but only coughed up blood before he fell back on the exam table.

"I'm going to fuck your throat, pop your cherry, and put a baby in you." Landry's threats bounced around in my head. Dropping the scalpel, I picked up the machete. "Joke's on you. My cherry was popped," I giggled. His eyes blinked. He'd suffered too much blood loss to elicit a greater reaction. "Boooo. You're no fun," I teased before I fisted his erect dick by the crown and swung the machete, cutting the appendage off like I was aiming to hit a grand slam. Landry definitely had a reason to be cocky. His dick was firmly above average in length and girth. "This probably explains why Addie was gagging for it."

I let the blade fall to the floor, holding Landry's most prized appendage in my hand. My pupils dilated, fascinated by how quickly his cock went limp. "I'd make some joke about you being a two-pump chump if I hadn't seen you're not with my own eyes," I said, moving back toward his head. I studied the cut along his throat. Landry's flaccid dick wouldn't fit. Dropping his cock on his chest, I reached up and pulled until there was enough room. "That should do it," I mumbled, then grabbed his dick and shoved it into his neck, pumping it in and out. "Who's fucking whose throat now?" I screamed. Blood splattered over my face, and I moaned. I almost wished Erebus was here so I could ride him.

Still not satisfied, I slipped my hand between my legs and pinched my clit.

Shame hit me at the realization of what I'd done. What they drove me to. Who they stole from me. All the pent-up rage of the night bubbled over. "Are you impressed with my game of operation? I had nothing to do with Vi's death. I was told she was missing," I yelled, looking for the camera before. Lodging Landry's cock into his throat, I spun around and stretched my arms wide. As I curtsied, I said, "You're welcome."

MINOS

I burst into the room. My mask was firmly in place. Harper was covered in blood. Seeing her like this made me want to fuck her, but she hadn't earned the right yet.

My brothers and I watched as she exacted her revenge. Erebus and Charon were enraptured. A behavior I expected from Erebus, but Charon was a surprise. My usually reserved brother whipped out his dick and jerked off while she fucked her boyfriend's throat with his own cock. I'd left after that, racing to catch the end in person, and missed it by a minute. I heard her say 'you're welcome' and laughed when Thanatos said she bowed. The fallen angel had spark. One we'd stoke the flames of.

"Congratulations. You've survived thus far," I said.

Harper Leigh glared at me. Her gray eyes lit like a California wildfire. "Can I go now?" she snarled, running her bloodied fingers through her hair. She was a beautiful mess.

"Not yet. There's still one more game to play," I smirked. She couldn't see it under the mask, which made it even more exciting.

Groaning, she retorted, "What the fuck else can be left? I didn't kill Viola. She was my best friend–the only true one I had."

I believed her. We all did. At first, when she'd pushed Adeline, I'd thought it was out of jealousy. That notion changed when her whispered confession sounded through the speakers in the control room. She didn't know we could hear even the slightest pin drop with the amount of mics and cameras outfitted in each area we led them through. That might be what got her out of here alive.

"If you can make it back to the gas station you passed when you arrived, we'll let you go."

Her lips thinned before she schooled her features, but she couldn't hide the hope and determination in her gaze. "So, I just need to get to the station? Nothing else? That's it?" She smartly questioned.

"All you need to do is run and try not to get caught," I stated.

Harper huffed, crossing her arms. "Like a game of tag," she mumbled.

"*Freeze* tag, if you will. Don't get caught, or you'll be at the mercy of your captor. They will decide what your punishment will be," I explained. "Oh, and Harper, no weapons. You automatically forfeit if we find you have anything from in this house."

Throwing her hair up in a messy bun, she clenched her teeth and scowled. "Fine! How long do I have?"

"You get a ten-minute head start. Make it back through the house and then the woods on foot. Do that, and you can leave." I lifted my hand and looked at my watch, waiting for the second hand to tick on the twelve. "But whoever catches you first gets to fuck you."

She prepared herself to run. Loosening up, she stretched and wiped the excess blood from her hands onto her pants.

"Your time starts," I began, waiting three seconds. "Now!"

Harper zipped past me, darting into the hallway. I enjoyed the view until she disappeared from sight before I shot a text for my brothers to meet me outside. We'd get there before she did. Backtracking was an indirect route to the front of the mansion.

Stepping outside, I inhaled the Louisiana fall air and headed for the woods. It was chilly since it was night. The perfect weather for a hunt. Once the blood started pumping, I'd welcome the cooler air.

I met my brothers as they stood on the hill outside the copse of trees. "Everything ready?" I inquired.

"All set," Charon responded.

"Perfect," I nodded.

It wasn't long before Harper Leigh appeared. The heavy sound of her footsteps grew louder as she approached. She didn't pause to take us in until she was at the entrance to the forest. She peered up, and my nostrils flared. I smelled her fear from here. Our imposing forms atop the hill, staring down like the four horsemen of the apocalypse, ready to end her world as she knew it. Harper glanced a moment longer before sprinting into the trees.

"God, her ass looks fantastic," Thanatos moaned, gripping his dick, and we all hummed our agreement.

We discussed the final parts of our plan when the alarm, signaling her ten-minute head start was up, went off.

"It's time," I commanded.

We took off down the hill in different directions. Erebus was the last person I heard before I ran out of sight.

"Run, little nightmare. Your demons are coming."

HARPER LEIGH

W here the fuck did the other one come from? I had seen a brief glimpse of guy number three earlier in the evening. I studied the four of them before sense reminded me I was on borrowed time.

It wasn't long before I heard branches snap, but I didn't look back. I was so close to freedom. "Whoever catches you first gets to fuck you." The words echoed in my head as I continued running, my aching muscles pumping. Being ravaged by the four men was the least of my problems.

Deep inside, I knew if they caught me, it was the end. There was a real possibility that they would kill me and I would end up just like my friends. Dead. My body left in the woods for animals and insects to scavenge. They wouldn't allow me to go back to my peaceful life and pretend like it was all a nightmare, something my brain had conjured from watching too many horror movies.

And they definitely wouldn't let me go to the police. Would the authorities even believe my story? The entire scenario was so far-fetched. Receive an invitation to a haunted house, fight for my life, survive a pool of acid and fireballs, have my virginity taken by a gun . . . Kill my frenemy and boyfriend. It was probably better if I didn't tell anyone what had happened.

The trees enveloped me, removing me from the world and clearing my thoughts. All I had to do was make it to the gas station. That was what Jack, the man who wore the horned mask, had said. It was the shop I had been turned away from earlier, but if she saw the condition I was in, surely she would take pity on me. I looked like hell, with cuts, bruises, and burns covering my flesh. Landry's blood still coated my skin, the rain unable to wash all of it away.

If I managed to live, the first thing I wanted to do was take a scalding shower and scrub all evidence of the night from me.

My heart pounded beneath my ribs, the blood roaring in my ears, muffling everything else as I focused on the only thing that mattered. Survival.

The shop had been fifteen minutes down the road. How long would it take for me to run there? An hour? The muscles in my legs screamed at me as they pumped, taking me closer to my destination.

Lightning crashed overhead, and thunder shook the ground. The thicket provided me with shelter from the worst of the rain and the wind. What remained of my clothes was soaked and the weather should have chilled me. Despite that, the adrenaline that coursed through my veins kept me warm, urging me to run faster.

My lungs burned as brambles snagged my skin, cutting into me like a knife. I didn't dare stop, even though I couldn't hear footsteps around me any longer. Small branches caught in my hair and whipped at my body. The ground was slick from freshly fallen leaves, and I slid, my feet sinking into the mud.

Despite the thunder and ragged breaths, I thought I heard a twig snap to my left. I pivoted as fast as I could to the right, slipping. I landed on my knees, mud covering my legs and hands. A stick broke behind me, and I righted myself, not caring about my clothes. Just run. It was the mantra that kept me going, even though my body begged me to slow down.

Suddenly, the wind was knocked out of me from the left side, and I stumbled to the hard ground. I scrambled to stand again, but vicious hands grabbed my ankles, yanking me closer. When lightning streaked across the sky again, I glimpsed the monster that had me in his clutches.

It was the one whose mask had a butterfly dripping blood–it was both beautiful and terrifying. He was responsible for the burn on the side of Landry's face after he dragged him from the room earlier. I didn't trust my chances with him. Erebus would use me, but keep me safe.

This guy? I had no idea.

A scream ripped from my throat as I kicked at him, determined to be set free. The sound was born out of horror and frustration. As soon as I heard it. I knew I had potentially given away my location.

My heel landed against the mask with a thud, and the man's grip loosened. I struggled to get to my feet and take off again. From behind, his voice reverberated through the trees. "That's right, cher. Struggle. Show us how strong you are and how much you want to live. Maybe it will make Minos take pity on you."

Take pity on me? And who was Minos? Fuck them. The darkness that had been brewing inside of me begged to be set free. If I could, I would have sliced all of their throats for putting me through what they had. The chance of me taking down all four of them was slim. Instead, I focused on the only thing in my control—running.

Running until my body pleaded with me to stop, my side cramped from lactic acid. Running even when my limbs shook from the excess adrenaline and the ground rumbled beneath my feet. Running even though my arms and torso had abrasions from the shrubs and thorns in the thicket.

Strong arms wrapped around my torso and clutched me like a vise. "Let me go," I growled, pressing my nails into my assailant's arms like claws. I tried tearing at the skin beneath the wet fabric, but was met with a dark chuckle.

"I'll never let you go, little nightmare. Thanatos was right. Show us how much you want to live. Fight me, and my brother might let you walk away."

Erebus' voice was a balm to my soul, whatever fragments were left of it. "Fuck you," I said as I continued to struggle against him.

My front collided against the bark of a tree, irritating the skin of my chest. He pressed against my back, his warmth radiating into me. "You've already done that, remember?"

"I hate you," I whispered, my eyes stinging. I had been so close to escaping. Was my face wet from sweat, tears, or the rain? I couldn't tell.

His hand closed around my throat, and he squeezed gently, a reminder of who was truly in charge. He unbuttoned my jeans with his opposite hand, and his palm cupped my pussy. "That's not the truth, and somewhere deep inside, you know it."

His lips brushed along the column of my neck, coming to rest on my shoulder. "You wish you could hate me, Harper. You wish that your body didn't like the things that it does."

His fingers pushed the fabric of my panties to the side, and he thrust one finger inside me. It was still tender from earlier, but I whimpered at it sliding in and out. "The chase, the fear. It turns you on, just like me."

For emphasis, he rolled his hips, pressing his hard cock against my ass. "You should thank us for setting your demons loose to play. A man like Landry could never satisfy you," he whispered before biting down on my shoulder. Pain lanced through my skin before he flattened his tongue against the wound, soothing the sting.

My cheeks heated from his words and the sound of his fingers plunging in and out of my arousal. "Never," I responded, even as my thighs clenched, something deep inside me coiling tighter. Every pass of his hand hit a spot that made my body sing.

"Mmm. Really? If you had married Landry, what would the future have held for you? Sex you scheduled every Friday night where you stared at the ceiling, thinking of anything else while you waited for him to finish fucking you? A white picket fence?"

His teeth seared my skin again. "Admit that he never made you feel like this."

I kept my mouth shut, my hands digging into him, and stifled the noises growing inside of me. Even when my walls contracted around his fingers and wetness gushed down my thighs, I refused to acknowledge what he said. It was nothing but a physical reaction to his touch. Just biology, I reminded myself, even though the little voice in the back of my head told me that wasn't accurate.

Even if I hated it and hated him, he was right.

"That's okay, little nightmare. I'll keep your secrets for you, and we'll both know the truth." He whipped me around to where I was facing him. In the darkness, he was only a silhouette, massive and obscured by shadows. He yanked my pants down my legs and picked me up, forcing me to wrap my thighs around him.

He shoved us back into the tree, and my breath hitched. Out of all the men, I felt the safest around him. It was a false sense of security, dumb on my part, but I didn't think he would truly hurt me. Not like the others. Maybe he would use me once more and then let me go.

The sound of his zipper lowering made me close my eyes. I didn't want my captor to see what he did to me and the reaction he coaxed out of my body. "You can't hide from me, Harper," he murmured as he plunged inside me, his thick cock stretching me. From the angle he held me, everything felt deeper. The piercing on his dick heightened the experience. I never had sex before, but I knew this wasn't an average lay. "Look at me while I fuck you."

My eyes fluttered open, and I stared at the faceless man who had taken my firsts. Heat rose with each thrust and slap of our skin. I silently begged my body to cooperate and not show him how much I secretly enjoyed what he was doing to me.

My body didn't cooperate, and when a second shadow appeared in my periphery, rather than stop the impending orgasm, it urged it on. "That's right, Harper Leigh. Show Erebus what a good little whore you are for him," the second man said.

When electricity lit up the sky, I saw the hammer that decorated his mask and shivered. The fear and friction mingled with the dirty words being spoken elicited a response from me. I tumbled over the edge of bliss, my muscles quaking against the bark of the tree.

Another set of footsteps approached. "Help me bind her," he muttered. "Bitch kicked me in the face and the last thing I want is a broken nose."

"Please, no," I whispered to Erebus, hoping to appeal to something deep inside him. He didn't respond, instead sliding out of me. His cum trailed down my thighs as he held my biceps, pulling me from the tree. I dug my heels into the mud beneath my feet, but it didn't help.

They had taken plenty from me. My virginity, my boyfriend, the hope that my best friend was alive . . . my sanity. But it wasn't enough. It was like they wanted to own me completely and steal away the leftover shards of my soul. "Little nightmare," Erebus whispered in my ear. "Relax. Trust me."

And just like that, my fight was gone. I couldn't stop whatever was happening to me, but maybe Erebus would save me in the end and protect me from the worst of what they had planned. I just had to live.

My bra fell to the ground as coarse rope wrapped around my torso, between my breasts. The rope wound repeatedly around me, binding my arms to my chest. Rather than further ratchet up my pulse, it had the opposite effect. Instead, it gave me a sense of calm and clarity. A focus on what was important. Even if they used my body, they wouldn't have my heart. Nothing was left of it, anyway.

The man with a hammer on his mask stepped in front of me before pulling me down with him, forcing me to straddle his waist. His fingers ran through my hair before he leaned close to my ear. "My brother calls you little nightmare, and I wish I could see what he does," the unknown man whispered against my skin before shoving me down on his length. He was bigger than Erebus, and I hissed in a breath as he seated himself completely. He snapped his hips, allowing my pussy no time to adjust. The fullness straddled pleasure and pain, but I'd never felt more alive.

A fourth apparition finally appeared from deep in the shadows. I recognized him, even without seeing his face. Even when fingers plunged in alongside my mystery man's dick and spread wetness to the tight hole behind it, my attention was on the one who promised my freedom if I made it.

The man behind me spit, and liquid trailed down my crack. I swallowed hard, knowing what was next. The head of his cock notched against my ass, and I squeezed my eyes shut, waiting for the invasion. Erebus' hand wound around my hair, forcing my head back. My scalp stung from the tension and my throat felt tight. "Relax, cher. Let him in, or he'll rip you in half."

Slowly, the mystery man inched inside of me, and the pain was almost too much to bear. Fingers danced along my clit, slowly morphing the pain into pleasure and a feeling of fullness. The masked man with the horns stalked forward, his hand wrapped around his dick. He stroked himself, and I stared at the angry length, partially obscured by the night. "Open up, Harper. If you use your teeth, I'll end your life before you can flinch." Jack.

Begrudgingly, I cooperated, allowing him to push the head of his cock inside my mouth. He tasted salty and musky. Masculine. His skin was velvety smooth against my tongue. It was slow at first, the same as the men who were filling me completely.

And then, like some flip had been switched, their tempos increased. I was pushed and pulled in an expert fashion, our skin slapping against each other. Jack snapped his hips against my face, plunging into my throat. My eyes watered from the invasion and I gagged. His fingers pinched my nose, cutting off my breath and forcing me to swallow around him.

The pressure on my clit increased as his balls clapped against my chin. When he pulled out, I took a deep breath, hoping it would be enough to last me for his next assault.

My pussy tightened once again, and I desperately wanted to cling to something. My fingers itched to dig into the shoulders of one of the men using me or curl into Erebus' shirt. Instead, I was left to shudder limply, allowing them to keep me upright. Pleasure overtook my body, blurring my senses, and I whimpered around the cock in my mouth.

"You're doing such a good job," Erebus said as his fingers left my clit, pinching my nipples. Warmth flooded my chest at his praise, and it was almost easy to forget that he was a demon sent from hell.

The man who hadn't spoken plunged into my ass once more and stilled, liquid heat pulsating inside me. He slipped out without a word and disappeared into the thicket. No one commented on that or cared. He'd gotten what he wanted from me. Hopefully, it would be enough to keep me alive.

Jack growled and pulled out of my mouth, his hand pumping his length. "You haven't earned my cum yet," he told me. His motions were fast and angry. Jets of his cum landed on my face and chest. His fingers ran along the liquid, smearing it further into my skin.

The man beneath me bit my bound breast as he raised his hips twice more, and then clutched me like his life depended on it. "Let her go, Minos," he uttered before he buried his head in the crook of my neck. Typically, I would have seen the gesture as some warped type of affection, but I was too tired, and my brain was muddled.

"What if she goes to the police?"

"She won't. Trust me," he mumbled as Erebus toyed with the bindings surrounding my body.

Minos tucked himself back into his pants and crossed his arms over his chest. "Fine. One condition. If she makes it back to the Mirage, she's free. If we catch her again, she's ours to do what we want with."

The rope fell from my body, and I staggered to my feet, grabbing my bra from the muddy ground. A hand wrapped around my upper arm, and Erebus embraced me tightly. A flash of lightning illuminated the sky and lit up the crows on his mask. "Run, little nightmare, and don't let me catch you." He ran his thumb along my lip before taking a step back.

Run.

Maybe this time, I could escape. I could taste freedom on the tip of my tongue.

Harper Leigh

My entire body was numb as the wood line gave way, and the road appeared in my vision. "Thank fuck," I mumbled out loud. My naked limbs felt like lead as I clambered toward the asphalt.

I hadn't heard anyone following me for at least ten minutes, and a huge part of me just wanted to lie down. Take a short rest. I couldn't yet. Not until I was at the palm reader's shop.

Briefly, I wondered if she would turn me away once she saw my appearance. Most of the blood on my hands was gone, but a quick glimpse told me I looked like I was the lone survivor of a horror movie.

I snorted to myself, thinking it was fitting.

Rain poured down in sheets around me, but I ignored it. Even the lightning was enough to bring me out of the fatigue-induced stupor I was in. Still, my feet plodded along to my destination as quickly as my body would allow.

Occasionally, a car passed by, their headlights blinding me. No one stopped to help me, and I was tempted to flag them down. Sure, there were horror stories about people who picked up hitchhikers, but would any of them be as bad as what I had just escaped?

I doubted it. After all, if they weren't sending me through a gauntlet of axes or fireballs, I probably wouldn't flinch. Not now.

Finally, the building I had been seeking came into my line of sight. My pace picked up. Victory was in my grasp. Despite the exhaustion, I broke into a jog and let my blood pump through my veins.

I slowed as I approached, horrified by what I found. The businesses from earlier were gone, nothing more than a figment of my imagination. I fell to my knees and allowed my tears to flow freely as lightning crashed around me.

The neon lights from the shop were gone, and the windows were boarded up. Paint peeled on the exterior of the small building, and part of the roof was missing.

Even next door, the gas station was vacant. The pumps were completely rusted, and the windows were broken. The wind howled as I stared at the sight before me.

It really had been a mirage. Nothing more than an illusion my broken brain had held onto. The businesses had been empty for years, maybe decades.

A sob shook my chest, and I curled up on the concrete, allowing myself a moment of sorrow. Pebbles cut into my bare skin, but I didn't care. Even if I found somewhere to hide, how would I get back to New Orleans? I had left my phone at Toussaint Manor in a basket. The people I had called my friends were dead, and my father was long asleep.

All I wanted was a hot shower and to crawl beneath my sheets.

Gravel crunched beneath tires, and an engine idled several feet away from me. A car door slammed, and footsteps approached me slowly. "Miss, do you need some help?" a deep voice called.

Relief, however fleeting, rushed through my system at the sound of another human. I gazed up through blurred vision, noting the absence of a mask. The man was tall with chestnut hair that was slightly damp from the rain and the most captivating green eyes. He wore pressed black slacks and a black button-up shirt. Full lips and cheekbones that had been carved by the gods completed his features.

Carefully, he unbuttoned his jacket and handed it to me, a small act of kindness allowing me to cover up my battered, naked body. After that, he extended his arm, his brows furrowed with concern. "Let's get you out of the rain. The lightning has been pretty bad tonight."

Cautiously, I accepted his hand, noting it was warm beneath my touch. He lifted me from where I was seated and strode across the parking lot. "Where are you headed to?" he asked as he opened the car door.

I shivered and wrapped my arms around myself. "New Orleans. Can you drop me off at Archambault University? I'm a student there."

He nodded and turned up the heat. My eyes were heavy as my skin warmed. My savior didn't seem to be one for conversation, and I didn't exactly know what to say. Small talk didn't seem appropriate after what I had been through.

It seemed like fate that someone had happened upon me in an abandoned parking lot. Or like I had a guardian angel who had been napping, woke up, and decided it was finally time to step in. I opened my eyes, curious about my good Samaritan. Thick dark lashes hooded his eyes. "What's your name?" I asked him.

He hesitated for a moment. "Theo."

"I'm so sorry about your seats," I mumbled, embarrassed about the fact that they would need to be detailed after he dropped me off.

He waved his hand in the air, dismissing me. "It needed to be done next week, anyway."

He seemed as uncomfortable with the conversation as I was. I glanced around the small car, noting that everything inside seemed perfect. Orderly.

A tarot card hung from a chain on the rearview mirror, and a shiver skated down my spine. The tower. The picture was ominous and dark, with lightning striking the building. I averted my eyes to the floorboard. Something white peeked out from beneath my seat, and I grabbed the edge of it, curious about what it was. My hands dropped the item, flying to my mouth to cover it.

It was a white mask with a butterfly, its wings shedding blood.

"No, no, no," I repeated to myself before clutching the door. I fumbled with the handle, attempting to open it. The terror that had been absent clawed at my heart.

"Calm down, Harper Leigh. It's not what you think," the man commanded in a calm voice.

Calm? How could I be calm? They had caught me again.

I screamed and pounded at the window.

The car swerved to the shoulder and stopped as Theo sighed. "I hate that it's come to this," he mumbled as he wrapped a hand around my neck. He squeezed gently until black spots filled my vision. "Maybe you'll feel better when you wake up."

And everything faded to black.

About P.H. Nix

P.H. Nix is a up and coming romance author.

She's a lover of morally gray heroes and kick ass heroines.

When she isn't dreaming up another story for you to sink your teeth into or lost in the world of her favorite authors, she's raising her own kick ass heroine!

Follow me on social media to stay up to date on my latest projects. Find the links at www.authorphnix.com or join my Facebook reader group!

About Celeste Night

Celeste Night detests writing in third person , so....

I am a romance author living somewhere outside of Birmingham, AL with my husband, two children, two dogs, three cats, and a partridge in a pear tree. I studied psychology in undergrad and thought I was going to be a therapist. Even when I was young, I would weave crazy stories and as I grew older dabbled in fan fiction. I never imagined that I would write a novel, much less publish it, so the journey has been amazing!

My relationship with the infamous Mr. Night was ripped straight out of the pages of a book (complete with angst and drama) and one day I might fictionalize that. I love morally gray (sometimes morally black) men and memes. When I'm not plotting imaginary murders or dreaming up my next favorite book boyfriend, I enjoy reading and playing video games (looking at you Stardew Valley). My favorite holiday is Halloween and my favorite color is black. I love possums because I also wake up screaming each morning.

Follow me on social media to stay up to date on my latest projects. Find the links at www.celestenight.com or join my Facebook reader group!

Made in the USA
Las Vegas, NV
07 March 2024